"Do..
taming me...

"About taming you?" Abby echoed.

"I'm leaving. Soon. And I am not the perfect man."

She eyed him suspiciously. Had someone told him that one of the conditions of receiving her inheritance was that she marry?

"I don't think you're in any danger of being mistaken for a perfect man."

Now he looked insulted.

"Mostly," she added hastily, "because in my experience, there is no such thing."

He snorted. "I'm going to start looking for another place to live."

"Suit yourself."

"I will," he muttered.

"Though I must admit, I'd feel very safe at night if you were to stay," she said, then realized her mistake.

For the heat in his eyes suggested she would be far from safe while under the same roof with Shane McCall....

***

THE WEDDING LEGACY

Dear Reader,

I hope the long hot summer puts you in the mood for romance—
Silhouette Romance, that is! Because we've got a month chock-
full of exciting stories. And be sure to check out just how
Silhouette can make you a star!

Elizabeth Harbison returns with her CINDERELLA BRIDES
miniseries. In *His Secret Heir,* an English earl discovers the
American student he'd once known had left with more than
his heart.... And Teresa Southwick's *Crazy for Lovin' You*
begins a new series set in DESTINY, TEXAS. Filled with
emotion, romance and a touch of intrigue, these stories are
sure to captivate you!

Cara Colter's THE WEDDING LEGACY begins with
Husband by Inheritance. An heiress gains a new home—
complete with the perfect husband. Only, he doesn't know it
yet! And Patricia Thayer's THE TEXAS BROTHERHOOD
comes to a triumphant conclusion when *Travis Comes Home.*

Lively, high-spirited Julianna Morris shows a woman's
determination to become a mother with *Tick Tock Goes the Baby
Clock* and Roxann Delaney gives us *A Saddle Made for Two.*

We've also got a special treat in store for you! Next month,
look for Marie Ferrarella's *The Inheritance*, a spin-off from
the MAITLAND MATERNITY series. This title is specially
packaged with the introduction to the new Harlequin continuity
series, TRUEBLOOD, TEXAS. But *The Inheritance* then leads
back into Silhouette Romance, so be sure to catch the opening
act.

Happy Reading!

Mary-Theresa Hussey

Mary-Theresa Hussey
Senior Editor

Please address questions and book requests to:
Silhouette Reader Service
U.S.: 3010 Walden Ave., P.O. Box 1325, Buffalo, NY 14269
Canadian: P.O. Box 609, Fort Erie, Ont. L2A 5X3

Husband by Inheritance

CARA COLTER

SILHOUETTE *Romance*®

Published by Silhouette Books

America's Publisher of Contemporary Romance

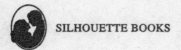

SILHOUETTE BOOKS

ISBN 0-373-19532-X

HUSBAND BY INHERITANCE

Copyright © 2001 by Cara Colter

This edition published by arrangement with Harlequin Books S.A.

Visit Silhouette at www.eHarlequin.com

Printed in U.S.A.

Books by Cara Colter

Silhouette Romance

Dare To Dream #491
Baby in Blue #1161
Husband in Red #1243
The Cowboy, the Baby and the Bride-to-Be #1319
Truly Daddy #1363
A Bride Worth Waiting For #1388
Weddings Do Come True #1406
A Babe in the Woods #1424
A Royal Marriage #1440
First Time, Forever #1464
*Husband by Inheritance #1532

*The Wedding Legacy

CARA COLTER

shares ten acres in the wild Kootenay region of British Columbia with the man of her dreams, three children, two horses, a cat with no tail and a golden retriever who answers best to "bad dog." She loves reading, writing and the woods in winter (no bears). She says life's delights include an automatic garage door opener and the skylight over the bed that allows her to see the stars at night.

She also says, "I have not lived a neat and tidy life, and used to envy those who did. Now I see my struggles as having given me a deep appreciation of life, and of love, that I hope I succeed in passing on through the stories that I tell."

Dear Reader,

I am not one of triplets, but I am one of three sisters. It wasn't until I was done writing the three books of THE WEDDING LEGACY that I realized how much I had borrowed in creating the characters. Abby is very much like my younger sister, Anna, in temperament: serene and strong and calm. Brittany has some similarities to my older sister, Avon: sexy, energetic and outgoing. (And she always wants to fix my hair!) I am the most like Corrine: creative and quiet, and always in jeans. I also can be a bit prickly to hide how sensitive I am!

My mom left my sisters and me a legacy, too. To her we owe an unfailing belief in the power of Love: to heal, to make whole, to make our world shine brighter.

That's my mom's legacy, and if the love I have for my sisters is able to reach out and embrace you, the reader, through these books, that would be the most wondrous of miracles.

This series is for all my sisters, everywhere.

Love,

Cara Colter

Prologue

"I'm sure it won't be much longer, Miss Blakely."

"Thank you," Abby murmured.

She looked around the lawyer's office uncomfortably. The furnishings were so rich—the coffee table in front of her dark walnut, the sofas soft, toffee-colored leather, the burgundy rugs deep and velvety, the lights muted.

Abby had never been in a lawyer's office before, and if a plane ticket hadn't been sent to her, she doubted she would be in one now.

Who would give a gift to her?

But that was what the registered letter had said. That she had been named as the recipient of a substantial gift, the donor anonymous. Her phone call to the law firm had gotten her no more information, just an invitation to be in the office of Hamilton, Sweet and Hamilton, in Miracle Harbor, Oregon, today, on February 15, at 10:00 a.m. precisely.

"Miss Blakely, are you sure you won't have coffee?"

The receptionist smiled kindly at her, and Abby knew she was doing a terrible job of hiding her discomfort. She knew she did not look like the kind of woman who belonged in these rich surroundings. Her wardrobe these days ran to things that washed easily. Clothes that she could wear in the sandbox or the playground, clothes that stood up to small handprints and grass stains and drool. And so she was wearing a casual skirt of stain-disguising navy blue, a matching tunic and a sweater jacket. She had made the ensemble herself for less than fifty dollars.

She caught her reflection in the highly polished wood of the coffee table, and patted her short blond hair self-consciously. Even the cut was about low maintenance rather than style.

She had been away from her just-turned-two daughter for less than twenty-four hours, and she felt as if a hole inside her heart was opening and getting wider by the minute. It was now almost ten-thirty.

"Is there a problem?" Abby asked. She looked wistfully at the door, sorry she'd been tempted to come here, sorry she'd accepted this odd invitation, knowing somehow her life was about to take an unexpected turn. Why now, when what she wanted most was a life without unexpected turns? A life of stability for her baby, Belle.

But that is why she had come here, too. Yes she was skeptical, but some small part of her hoped the gift would be something that would enable her to give her daughter exactly the life she wanted for her. A little house of their own, instead of the apartment. A nicer neighborhood, closer to a park. A new sewing machine so Abby could take in more work.

Counting her chickens before they hatched, she reprimanded herself. Still, she had been sent a plane ticket worth several hundred dollars. She had been picked up in Portland by a limo and deposited at Miracle Harbor's most luxurious hotel. And the letter had promised the ''gift'' was substantial.

Hope was what had made her cross the continent, from Illinois to this small hamlet in Oregon. Miracle Harbor. The town, built in a half moon on the hills surrounding a bay, was a place of postcard prettiness—neat rows of beautiful old shingle-sided houses behind white picket fences, rhododendrons growing wild, the air delightfully warm and scented of the sea.

''Is there a problem?'' she asked, again.

''No, of course not. We're just waiting for the arrival of the other parties.''

''The other parties?'' Abby asked, baffled. This was the first she had heard of other parties.

The receptionist suddenly was the one who looked uncomfortable, as if she had revealed more than was professionally acceptable.

So when the door swung open, both she and Abby looked to it with relief.

A woman stepped into the office, in dark glasses and a short fur jacket. A long skirt, shimmering jade-colored silk, swirled around her slender legs as she moved with a breezy self-confidence into the room. Her hair was beautifully coiffed, and yet a hint of something wild remained in the way it swung, electric, around her shoulders.

There was something so familiar about her, Abby thought, frowning, and then realized the woman must be almost exactly her own size and height. Even her hair color was familiar, tones of wheat mixed with honey.

''Hi. I'm Brittany Patterson. I—''

As she caught sight of Abby out of the corner of her eye, her voice froze. She swung around and stared. Her mouth opened, then closed, then opened again. Slowly, she lifted the sunglasses off her eyes, and Abby felt the blood drain from her face, thought for an awful moment that she was going to faint.

Because the face she was looking at was the very same face she looked at in the mirror each day.

The makeup was bolder, the eyebrows more carefully shaped, this woman lovelier somehow, and yet identical to her in every way.

The door swung open again, and Abby turned to it in relief, needing a distraction from the intensity of emotion, the confusion welling up within her.

Another woman entered the office, breathless, as different from the woman in the fur jacket as night from day. She was in jeans and a jean jacket, both faded nearly white, her long hair swept back off her face in a careless ponytail.

Different from the other woman, except in one way.

Her face was identical. And so was her shade of hair. And the striking hazel of eyes nearly blue, except for a star of brown around the pupil.

As if in a dream, Abby got up from the deep sofa. Moved toward the other women, and then began to shake. She sat back down. Silently, the other women came and sat down, too, looking at each other with an astonishment deeper than words.

The receptionist was bringing them all coffee now. Abby might have laughed to see each of the other women get their coffee ready just as she did—a tiny splash of cream, three sugars, and then a soft blow on the hot liquid—except that it was too bizarre to be funny.

"Well," said the one in the fur, finally breaking the stunned silence, "unless we're on *Candid Camera,* I'd guess we're related."

"More like *The Twilight Zone,*" the one in the jean jacket said, and then all three of them laughed. The two young women's voices, though they had different regional accents, were identical in tone and pitch. Abby recognized her own voice when they spoke.

And then they were all talking at once.

"Did you have any idea? I knew I was adopted but—" Abby's voice was shaking.

"I knew I was adopted," the one in the fur coat said, "but I didn't know I had sisters."

"I was never adopted," the jean-clad woman said, her voice hesitant. "I lived with my Aunt Ella until I was ten. She said my parents—our parents?—were killed in a car crash."

"It's clear we are more than sisters. We must be triplets," the one in the fur coat announced, and they stared at each other, thrilled and shocked and astonished. "I'm Brittany."

"Abigail. Abby." She could hear the catch of emotion in her voice.

"Corrine. Corrie."

The receptionist interrupted. "Mr. Hamilton will see you now."

They followed her down the hall into an office, glancing at each other with speculative delight, with wonder.

Mr. Hamilton was a dignified man, his manner and dress authoritative. Silver hair and deep wrinkles around his eyes made him look as if he should be retired. He looked genuinely amazed as the three identical young women entered his office and took seats across from him.

"I'm sorry," he said. "Pardon me for staring. I—I didn't know. You all had different last names. I had no idea—"

He looked down at the papers in front of him, struggling for composure. When he looked up he studied them each in turn.

"Triplets," he finally concluded. "Had you ever met each other?"

When they shook their heads, he looked very grave. "I'm sorry. I would have never popped this kind of surprise on you without warning you. I can't imagine what she was—" His voice faded, and then he cleared his throat. "As you know from the letter you received, I have asked you here because my client wishes to bestow a gift on each of you."

"Who is your client?" Brittany asked, and Abby noted she seemed far more comfortable in the rich surroundings than either of her sisters.

"I'm not at liberty to say. I have been given a letter to read to you." He took a paper off his desk, held the letter way back and squinted at it.

"Dear Abigail, Brittany and Corrine," he read in a rich baritone, "Many years ago, I made a promise to your mother. She died within minutes of extracting that promise from me. To my shame, it was a promise I was unable to keep. I have reunited you with your sisters in the hope this gesture will begin to make the amends I owe your mother and each of you. I have also given you each a gift that I hope will turn out to be the very thing you most need in your lives. My attorney, Mr. Jordan Hamilton, will outline the nature of each gift, and the conditions I have attached to it. My wish is for your every happiness."

"What was the promise she made to our mother?"

Abby asked, hungry to know any detail that would help her come to grips with this overwhelming set of circumstances.

"I'm afraid, aside from the gifts, and the attached conditions, I don't know any more than what is in the letter," Mr. Hamilton said.

"Conditions?" Brittany asked skeptically. "You might as well get to that first."

"All right. In order for you to receive your gifts, permanently, you must remain here in Miracle Harbor for a period of one year." He cleared his throat uncomfortably. "And you must marry within that year."

Abby stared at him. So, it was a joke after all. It had to be. But he looked perfectly serious.

She shot a look at her sisters.

Brittany looked indignant, Corrine was looking out the window, her thoughts masked. Except for some reason, Abby knew exactly what she was feeling. Corrie was scared to death.

"The gifts?" Brittany said, narrowing her eyes at him, and folding her arms across her chest. "And this had better be good."

He gave her a stern look, rattled his papers, then, beginning with Abby, he told them about the most astonishing gifts....

Chapter One

After all these years, he still slept as though there was a possibility of someone sneaking in the room and putting a gun to his ear.

Even in Miracle Harbor, Oregon, where such things were unheard of.

He lay awake, now, listening, every muscle tense, ready, wondering what small noise had startled him awake in the deepest part of the night. The green glow of his clock told him it was just after 3:00 a.m.

The foghorn, he decided, not the creak of his front gate, badly in need of oiling. He allowed himself to relax slightly, and then slightly more, closing his eyes and willing himself to go back to sleep. He hated this time of night the most because he was unable to exercise his customary discipline over his mind. For some reason this was when the memories wanted to visit.

The sound came again.

The quiet crunch of someone's muffled footsteps moving up the walk. He listened for and heard the scrape of the loose board on the second step up to the porch.

It was when he heard the soft groan of his front door handle being tried that he moved, fast and quiet, out of the his bed and to the window.

An old car, hitched to a U-Haul trailer, was parked out on the street. Thieves? Planning to clean him right out?

They'd be disappointed. He had no interest in "stuff." His apartment was Spartan. No TV, no stereo, just his computer.

Had he once had an interest in "stuff"? He had trouble remembering small things like that. Though he had a flash now of his wife, Stacey, standing in front of something in a store, looking back at him, laughing at the outrageous price, but there had been something wistful in her eyes, too.

He flinched as if he'd been struck when he remembered what they had been looking at that day.

A bassinet.

A blackness that did not bode well for his intruder, descended over him. Wearing only the boxers he slept in, he made his way down the steps and through the darkened house, the of movement—stealthy, cautious, icily calm—second nature to him.

He slid out the back door, not opening it enough to let it squeak, his plan already formed. He'd use the walkway alongside the house and follow it to the front. The prowler would be trapped on the narrow porch. He'd have to go through him to get away.

Fat chance of that.

This intruder had picked the wrong house.

Home of Shane McCall, agent, Drug Investigation Unit. Retired.

The mist was thick and swirling, the cement of the sidewalk ice-cold under his bare feet, the rhododendrons so thick along the side path that his bare skin was brushing the rough shingles of his house on one side, and getting soaked by the rubbery leaves on the other. These details barely registered, he was so intensely focused. He came around the side of the house, stopped in the shadow of the fog and dense overgrown shrubs, and watched.

He saw a shape bent over the door; the night too dark and the fog too thick for more than vague impressions. A baseball cap. A build too slight to be threatening to him.

A kid, he thought, and felt his anger wane as he watched the intruder jiggle the door handle again. Was he trying to pick the lock? Shane should have just called the police. Maybe Morgan was working tonight. When the business was done they could have exchanged war stories.

Vastly preferable to going back up those stairs to bed when he'd finished here, to the memories that were waiting for him.

Knowing that calling the police was still an option, and knowing he wouldn't take it, he moved quietly out of the shadows to the bottom of his steps.

It occurred to him that maybe he should have taken his service revolver out of retirement, that someone without the physical size to handle a confrontation might attempt to even out his odds with a weapon. A knife, a handgun. That was probably especially true of the kind of kid who would break into a house at three in the morning.

His mind working with that rapid, detached lightning swiftness that came naturally to him, Shane decided on a course of action—keep his distance, make it seem like he was packing a gun himself.

Hard to do, considering he was standing out here in his undershorts. But not impossible.

He went to the bottom of the stairs, and with the cold authority that came so easily to him, he said, "Put your hands up where I can see them. Don't turn around."

The figure bolted upright and then froze.

"You heard me. Hands up."

"I can't." Fear had made the voice high and girlish.

"You can't?" he said, his voice cool and hard. "You'd better."

"I might drop the baby."

The voice was so scared that it was quivering. *The baby?*

Shane went up the steps two at a time, put his hand on intruder's shoulder and spun him around.

Her.

Two hers, a full-grown her, and a baby her, both looking at him with the same saucer-huge blue eyes. Blue eyes tinged with a hint of brown.

He dropped his hand from her shoulder, ran it through the dampness of his hair, and swore.

When her foot connected with his shin, he was reminded, painfully that he had forgotten rule one: never let your guard down *ever.*

"Fire," she screamed. "Fire."

Without thinking he clamped his hand over her mouth before she managed to roust the whole neighborhood, something he was not exactly dressed for.

She was beautiful. Blond hair, very short and straight, poking out from under a Cubs ball cap and framing a face of utter loveliness—perfect skin, high cheekbones, a shapely nose. Her eyes were her dominating feature, though. Huge, the color partly a sea blue he had only seen once, a long time ago, off the coast of Kailua-Kona, in Hawaii, and partly brown. The combination was nothing short of astounding.

Those eyes were sparkling with unshed tears.

He swore again. She was shaking now, and the baby looked anxiously at her mother, screwed up her face and began to howl.

The noise seemed to reverberate in the fog, and he glanced uneasily at the neighbor's houses again.

"Promise you won't scream," he said. "Or yell fire." Fire. All right. She was beautiful, but obviously deranged.

She nodded.

He moved his hand fractionally, and she backed away from him until she could back away no more, her shoulder blades right up against his front door, her eyes wide, her arms folded protectively around the baby. It wasn't a small baby. In fact, she was quite sturdy looking, possibly two.

"Stay away from us, you pervert."

"Pervert?" he sputtered. "Pervert?"

"Hiding in the bushes in your undershorts waiting for a defenseless woman to come home. That's called a pervert."

"Home?" He stared at her. Her voice was shaking but her eyes were flashing. She probably weighed less than him by at least eighty pounds. And he knew she was going to take him on if he came one step closer.

She nodded, licked her lips nervously. Her eyes darted by him, looking for an escape.

He folded his arms over his chest. "This happens to be *my* home. I thought *you* were a prowler."

Her mouth fell open, and then her eyes narrowed with suspicion.

He could *see* what she was thinking: that perverts were damnably clever. But he could also see the confusion in her face, her eyes searching for and finding the black iron house number over the wall-mounted porch light.

He was not sure he'd ever been quite so insulted. A pervert? Him? And she didn't seem really deranged. Just exhausted. He could see dark crescents bruising the skin under those beautiful eyes.

She studied him a moment longer, and then he could see some finely held tension ease slightly.

"Oh, God," she said. "I've made a mistake. I'm very tired. I—"

To his horror, little tears were slipping down her cheeks now, too. She wasn't wearing any mascara, which he liked for some foolishly irrational reason. Her shoulders were shaking under a jacket that looked too thin to offer any kind of protection from the penetrating chill of the night.

The baby's howls intensified when she saw the tears dribbling down her mother's cheeks.

Striving for dignity, the woman pulled back her shoulders, lifted her chin. The gestures wrenched oddly at a heart that he would have sworn, only moments ago, had been cast in pure iron.

"Could you just direct me to a motel?"

"I could, but you won't have any luck." This did not seem to surprise her. "Why fire?"

"Pardon?"

"You yelled fire," he reminded her. "Are perverts scared of it? Like holding a cross up to a vampire?"

She laughed nervously. "I read once that nobody lis-

tens when a woman calls for help. But they will if someone calls fire.''

She wasn't from around here, he decided. Not even
close. Survival tactics of a big city woman. Her voice
was intriguing. It wasn't sweet, like her face. It had a
little raspy edge to it.

"Why aren't there any motels? There were 'No Va-
cancy' signs on every motel for the last fifty miles it
seemed.'' She wiped impatiently at her eyes with the
back of her sleeve, and then wiped the baby's face, and
kissed her on the nose.

A magical effect. The baby, an exact replica of her
mother, except with blonder hair that was, wildly curly
and unruly, ceased howling. The girl turned her head
enough to look solemnly at him out of the corner of
one eye, but apparently the glance failed to reassure,
and she began to cry again, louder than before.

"There's a major resort going up on the edge of
town. We have contractors, carpenters, plumbers...you
name it they're here.''

He doubted there was a room to be had anywhere
this night.

Unless you counted his empty house. Three bedrooms. One up, two down. The place had been a duplex
until a few months ago when, with his landlord's permission, he had turned the upstairs kitchen into a work-
room.

Don't, he told himself.

But he did, feeling slightly put out that he'd fright-
ened her so badly, but even more put out that the baby
was going to wake up the whole bloody neighborhood.

"Look, maybe you better come in for a minute.''

He reached past her for the door. Which was locked.
The baby's crying was affecting him so badly, he con-

sidered a well-placed kick to the old wood, but contained himself.

"No," she said, firmly, her suspicion leaping back in her eyes. "I'm leaving. It's all right. Really. I'm tired. I drove too long. I must have the wrong address."

She went to move by him and then stopped, the porch opening onto the stairs too small for her to squeeze by without touching him. It was when he saw the delicate blush rising in her cheeks that he remembered he was in a state of undress.

"Wait right here," he said sternly, using his no-nonsense cop voice, a man to be taken seriously, even in his underwear. Boxers, thank God. The plaid kind that could be mistaken for a pair of gym shorts in a thick fog. Maybe.

She was scared still, it was written all over her face.

Scared that if he was not a pervert that had been hiding in the bushes, she had accidentally knocked on the door of Miracle Harbor's only axe-murderer.

"I'm a cop," he said reluctantly, "Retired." He knew she'd see it. The stance, the look in his eyes, the cut of his hair.

Her eyes wide on his face, she nodded, then as soon as he stepped back, she flew by him, and scurried down the walk. He let her go, listening to the snap of the locks on her car doors when she was safely inside it.

Then he listened to the unhealthy grind as she turned the ignition.

Not his problem, he thought, at all. Thank God.

He went back down the sidewalk, and in his back door. He ordered himself up the steps and into bed. He made it up the steps, but his mind, never disciplined at this time of night, listened for the sound of the car pulling away. Nothing.

He opened his window, took a look out, and heard again the grind of the starter.

"Hell," he said, and picked up a pair of jeans off the end of his bed. "Double hell."

Despite a shin that should have told him otherwise, the woman had a vulnerable quality in her eyes. He wanted to leave her to her fate, and couldn't. She wasn't dressed warmly enough to be sitting out there in a freezing car, and the child probably wasn't either.

Minutes later, snapping up his jeans, he turned on the porch light and flung open the front door.

She could come in if she wanted to.

But she didn't.

Stubborn. That was written all over her face. Beautiful, yes, but stubborn, too. He snuck a glance out the door.

The wind lifted the fog enough for him to see her. She had her forehead resting against the steering wheel. She was probably crying. But she wasn't going to ask for his help. Not him. The pervert.

Sighing, he pulled a jacket over his naked chest. He'd taken an oath, years ago, to protect and serve. And retired or not, that oath was as much a part of his makeup as anything else. It ran through his blood, and he found himself almost relieved at the discovery that his personal tragedy had not stolen that part of his nature from him.

He was not capable of leaving her out there in the cold.

She didn't see him coming, and started when he tapped on her window. There, he'd managed to scare her again, which should warn him to give up any notion of a new career in the damsel-in-distress department.

She opened her window a crack. "Yes?"

"Do you want me to call somebody for you? Have you got road service?" Old habits died hard. Her license plates said Illinois. There was a parking sticker on her windshield for a lot in Chicago. He'd been right when he guessed this woman was a long way from home.

"I'll be fine," she said proudly. "In Chicago this is picnic weather."

"Yeah," he said. She was shivering. "I can see that. Is that baby as cold as you are?"

She gave the child a distressed look, and turned back to him. "Are you really a police officer?"

"I was, yes."

"Have you got a badge?"

"Not anymore."

"Why aren't you a policeman anymore?"

His aggravation grew. It occurred to him it was the most he'd felt of anything for a long, long time. He actually felt alive. Aggravated, but alive.

"Lady," he said, "are you going to make me beg you to come in?"

She seemed to mull that over, then with a resigned sigh, she undid the lock and reached for the baby. She followed him up the walk.

He held open the door for them. The baby was nestled into her mother's chest now, sucking her thumb. When she glanced at him, she scrunched up her face again, and opened her mouth so wide he could see her tonsils.

The baby was wearing a knitted sweater with a little pink hood and pom-poms.

A memory niggled, so strong, so hard, he nearly shut the door.

Their baby was going to be a girl. The amniocentesis

*had told them that. Stacey had begun to buy pink things.
Little dresses. Booties.*

"Are you all right?" the woman asked him.

*No. He wasn't. Two years, and he still wasn't. He
had accepted it now. That he was never going to be all
right. That time would not heal it.*

But he lied to her. "Sure. Fine. Come in."

She stepped hesitantly over the threshold. The baby
craned her neck and looked around.

"I'm Abby Blakely," she said, and freeing a hand,
extended it. She was small, but in the full light, she
looked older than she had outside. Mid to late twenties.
Not the teenager the Cubs cap had suggested. Her figure
was delectable—slender, but soft in all the right places.

He took her hand, noting for a hand so small, it was
very strong. "Shane McCall."

"And you really were a policeman?"

"Why do you find that so hard to believe?"

"It's not the policeman part I find hard to believe.
It's the retired part."

"Oh."

"You don't look very old."

The mirror played that trick on him, too. He looked
in it and saw a man who looked so much younger than
he felt.

"Thirty," he said.

"Surely you're a little too young to be retired, Mr.
McCall?"

"Shane. Uh. Well. Semi, I guess. I'm a consultant
on police training, now. Look, do you want to come in
and sit down?"

Her eyes found his ring finger, and he saw her register the band of soft, solid gold that winked there. "Are
we going to wake your wife?"

"No. I'm a widower."

"I'm sorry." After a moment, "You seem young for that, too."

"Tell God." He heard the bitter note in his voice, and would have done anything to erase it. "Look, are you coming in or not?"

She hesitated, looked like she was going to cry again, wiped at her face with her sleeve. "I don't know what I want to do. I'm so tired." She brightened. "I know, I'll call one of my sisters."

He liked the way she said *sister*, somehow putting so much love into the word that he knew her sister wouldn't mind her calling at this time of the night. But why hadn't she thought of that before?

She thrust the baby at him and bent to undo her shoes. It seemed to him he'd been in a better position when she didn't trust him. He wasn't good with babies.

He held the chubby body awkwardly, at arm's length. "Uh, just leave your shoes on."

"On these floors. Are you crazy?"

He looked at the floors, not sure he'd ever noticed them before. Wood. In need of something. Tender loving care.

The baby was regarding him with a suspicious scowl. Like mother, like daughter. "Me, Belle," she finally announced warily.

"Great. Hi." He still held her out, way far away from him.

She wiggled and he could feel the lively energy, the strength in her.

Abby straightened, and he went to hand the baby back. "Could you just hold her for a minute? Just until I use the phone?"

It would seem churlish to refuse. "The phone's

through here," he said, leading the way, past the closed door that went into the empty main floor suite, and down the hall to the kitchen. The baby waggled away on the end of his held-out-straight-in-front-of-him arms.

"She won't bite you."

"Oh." He made no move to change his position. Belle wiggled uncomfortably.

"Does she smell?" Abby asked.

"Belle no smell," the baby yelled indignantly.

"Uh," he managed to unbend his arms a little, draw the baby into him. Sniffed. She did smell. Of heaven. Something closed around his heart, a fist of pain.

And whatever emotion it was, it telegraphed itself straight to the baby, because she stared at him round-eyed, then touched his cheek with soft fingers, took the collar of his jacket in a surprisingly strong grip, and pulled herself into him.

"That's otay," she told him, nestling her blond curls under his chin and her cheek against his collarbone, and beginning to slurp untidily on her thumb. Drool fell down the vee of the jacket he hadn't taken off for fear of reoffending Ms. Blakely's sensibilities with the view of his naked chest.

"The phone's right there."

His intruder gave his kitchen, which was as Spartan as his bedroom, a cursory glance, went to the phone and picked it up. He could hear her calling information. How come she didn't have her sisters' phone numbers?

When she hung up she looked discouraged again.

"They're not here yet. My sisters."

"Here yet?"

"We're all moving here. It's a long story." She looked exhausted and broken.

"All? Like how many dozen are you talking?"

She laughed a little. "Just three. I'm one of triplets."

Three of her. That was kind of a scary thought for a reason he didn't want to contemplate. The baby was sleeping against his chest, snoring gently. He registered the warmth of her tiny body, the light shining in her curls, and braced himself, waiting for some new and unspeakable pain to hit him.

"I'll call a road service for you," he said, tight control in his voice, "But I wouldn't count on anything happening right away. This isn't Chicago."

She looked at him, startled.

"License plates," he said. "Parking sticker on the left-hand side of your windshield."

"You really are a cop."

"Not now," he corrected her.

Still leaving him with the baby she began to fish through a bag nearly as big as she was. She came out finally, triumphant, with a piece of wrinkled paper.

She handed it to him.

He awkwardly shifted "Me-Belle" to the crook of his arm and took the piece of paper. He stared at it. Blinked rapidly. Looked again. His own address was written there in a firm, feminine hand.

"There's some mistake," he finally said.

"Why?"

"This house is number twenty-two, Harbor Way."

She looked deflated. "I must have written it down wrong."

"You must have."

She slumped down on a chair, took off her ball cap, ran a hand through her straight hair. It was sticking up in the cutest way. "Now what? I have to go. Obviously."

That was obvious all right. Her hair was tangled and

damp, and her face was pale with weariness. And still, all he could think, was that she was damnably sexy. She was wearing jeans that were way too big for her, accentuating the fact she was as slender as a young willow. She couldn't stay here. Obviously.

"Look, for what's left of tonight, you can stay here," he heard himself saying. "The house actually used to be two self-contained units. It also used to be a summer rental. It's all furnished. There's linens in the closets. I've never even used the bedrooms down here. They're across the hall."

"You're a complete stranger!"

"I admit it. Stranger than some."

She managed a small, tired smile.

"There's a lock on the door. Not that I'm in the habit of attacking people. In my underwear."

He could tell that clinched it. The lock. Not his reassurances. The lock and the fact that she was tired beyond words and probably close to collapse.

"Thank you," she said softly.

"Whatever. In the morning, I'll help you get your car straightened away, and find your house."

"Shane?"

"Yeah?" He wished she wouldn't have called him his first name. He didn't want to be her friend. He didn't even want to be her rescuer. He just didn't have any choice.

"You're making me very sorry I kicked you so hard."

From behind the locked door, Abby listened to Shane go up the stairs, and wondered if she'd lost her mind. Not only had she packed every earthly possession that she cared about and trekked across a whole country with her baby, now she was under the same roof as a man she knew nothing about.

Well, not nothing exactly.

He had been a cop.

And she had never in her life seen eyes like that. It wasn't the color, precisely, though the dark chocolatey brown was enormously attractive; it was the look in them. Intense, the gaze steady and strong and stripping.

It was those eyes that had kept panic from completely engulfing her when he had come up behind her as she tried to make her key fit in the front door. *His* front door.

While part of her had been screaming in pure panic— *near-naked man lurking in the bushes at three in the morning*—another part of her had registered those eyes and told her that the hard beating of her heart might not have a single thing to do with fear.

Naturally, she wasn't going to listen to that part of herself. She was resigned to the fact that she was not a good judge of masculine character. Belle's father being a case in point. Still, even when she'd been desperately trying to think of how to get by that formidable man who had trapped her there on that tiny porch, some traitorous little part of her had been staring at him in awe.

Registering every detail of him. His height, the width of his shoulders, the smooth unblemished skin, the clinging night mist showing off his impressive physique as surely as if he was a bodybuilder, oiled.

Because he had been tense, geared for action, he had seemed to be all enticing masculine hardness. Mounded pecs, the six-pack stomach, the ripple of sinew and muscle in his arms and legs.

She shouldn't have been so surprised when he'd said

he used to be a cop, because he had policeman hair—
the cut short, neat and very conservative and the color
of cherry wood. And there had been a certain authoritative hardness in his face, too. A look of readiness in
the taut downturn of his mouth, the narrow squint of
his eyes. He was a man who was prepared to do battle.

It was probably that strength, a core-deep thing, that
had convinced her to take a chance and trust him. Her
instincts told her that of all the places she could choose
to stay tonight, admittedly limited, she would not find
one safer than this.

Her adopted mother would, of course, be horrified.
Poor Judy wanted life to be so neat and tidy. She had
worked so hard to give Abby a decent home, even
though she herself had been a single mother.

Judy had thought it was insane to go to the lawyer's
office, even more insane to accept the gift. What would
she think of this latest twist?

The situation tonight, Abby reminded herself, had
been desperate. What else was she going to do? Sleep
in her car? If it was just herself, that might have been
okay. But with Belle? It was a terrible night out there,
damp and cold. Even her mother would understand why
she had chosen to stay here. Wouldn't she?

Abby went unseeingly through the plainly furnished
apartment, found the first bedroom, lay her sleeping
daughter in the center of the big double bed, and went
to pull the drape. As she did, she realized she was facing
the street. Miracle Harbor didn't look at all like it had
looked when she'd been here a month ago. It had looked
so beautiful then, with its quaint, weathered houses lin-
ing steep, narrow avenues that all led to the ocean. The
main street had redbrick shops, with colorful awnings,

big picture windows looking out on the beach and the ocean they fronted.

Tonight, with the swirling mist, it looked more like a scene out of a horror movie, set in the fog-shrouded streets of Gothic London.

How could she have written down the address of the house she had inherited incorrectly? How could she?

And how could a town that had looked so cheery and welcoming in the light of day look so distinctly formidable at night?

And how could her traitorous car just give up like that? Of course, it was old, and she had asked a lot of it, carrying her across the country dragging all her earthly possessions along behind it. Maybe it was a miracle that it had made it this far before it had quietly quit.

Miracles, she thought, and turned from the window. She checked the corners and under the bed for spiders or webs, and finding none, tumbled into the bed beside her daughter, too tired to find the bedding. Miracles, she thought again with a sigh. Isn't that why she had come here, really?

Some part of her wanted to believe, more than anything else, that this old world could still work a miracle or two.

She thought of the conditions of her inheritance, the inheritance that would allow her to give her daughter everything she wanted for her. A home, a safe place to grow up.

If you didn't count perverts in the bushes. She giggled tiredly at the thought.

Of course, there were those conditions. One to live here in Miracle Harbor for at least a year. No problem. But two?

Preposterous. How could someone get married just for personal gain? What kind of marriage would that be? And given her history with Ty, Belle's dad, she simply knew she couldn't trust herself in the all important department of mate selection.

So, why had she come, uprooted her whole life, knowing she had no intention of fulfilling that second condition?

During her brief visit with her sisters, she had learned they had been separated at about age three. She had no memory of them, but Corrine said she had foggy memories of something. And Brit's adoptive parents had told her she was three when she came to them.

Abby had come because she wanted to know her sisters better, *had* to know them, had felt as soon as she had seen them, a deep sense of having found herself.

And maybe, in some small, lost part of herself, she really wanted to believe in fairy-tale endings, wanted to believe in a place with a name like Miracle Harbor, maybe she could expect anything to happen.

Maybe it had already started, with her at the wrong house, and the car not starting, all things linked together, part of a larger plan.

For her.

And what about him? How would he fit into that plan?

He wouldn't. He'd done the decent thing tonight, she suspected because his training would allow him to do nothing else.

By tomorrow, he would be part of her history, somebody she could nod to when she passed him on the street.

There had been mile-high barriers in that man's cool

eyes, and she felt no desire to try and penetrate that mystery.

But even if she did decide to try and fulfill that ridiculous condition placed on her gift, she would never pick a man like him. She wanted someone sweet and kind. Someone who would make a good father for her daughter.

A little pudgy fellow with glasses, who took lunch in a paper bag to his office.

Upstairs, she heard the groan of a bedspring, and felt the oddest little stir in her stomach. A stir that a little pudgy fellow with glasses would never be able to create.

Which was just as well. That stir, she knew, led to nothing but trouble.

Chapter Two

A streak of sunshine had crept through a crack in the drape, and lay in a stripe across her face, making her blink lazily awake. Abby stretched luxuriously, looked around the room. Even in the full light of day there was not a spiderweb in sight.

The furnishings were plain, in keeping with what Shane McCall had said about the house being a summer rental, but the room itself was lovely. High, plastered ceilings, wood floors, wide oak window casings.

Would the house that had been given to her as a gift by a complete stranger be as beautiful?

She thought of last night, and Shane McCall, and she felt, again, that funny little shiver of pure awareness.

"Abby," she told herself. "You are now rested. You are immune to that man. You know the truth about another pretty face. Isn't that right, darlin'?"

She reached out to pull her daughter to her, reached further, patted the mattress, and as the awful truth sank in, she sat bolt upright in bed. Only a little dent remained where her daughter had slept snugly beside her last night.

"Belle," she called, leaping from bed, "where are you?" She fumbled for buttons on her homemade blouse that had sprung undone during the night, trying to keep the panic out of her voice. This place wasn't child-proofed like her modest apartment in Chicago. "Belle?"

She raced into the next room. A chair had been pulled up to the door, the kind that had the twist style of lock on the handle. The door was now open into the hallway that led to the outer door and the kitchen they had been in last night.

Did the door to the outside have the same kind of lock? Abby tried to think from last night. She was sure the lock she had tried to fit her key into was a deadbolt. Even her precocious daughter would have trouble with that.

But, as she scrambled into the hallway, her heart sank. The front storm door wasn't locked. It wasn't even closed, a brisk, sea-scented breeze coming in through the screen.

"Belle!"

"In here."

Only it wasn't Belle who answered. It was him, his voice loaded with irritation.

She catapulted into the kitchen, and skidded to a halt. *Immune,* she reminded herself.

But really that rush of relief that her daughter was here and not happily exploring the streets of Miracle Harbor, getting closer and closer to the ocean, seemed to have lowered her defense system again.

She was suddenly not sure she had registered his full impact last night. Just looking at him made her feel hot and flustered, like a woman who had a sign flashing on her forehead that said: I Need A Husband. Desperately.

He was a man who didn't seem to like much clothing. This morning he had on navy blue running shorts that showed off tanned, muscular legs, and a flat, hard fanny. A grey sweatshirt with some sort of police emblem on it stretched tight over the broadness of his chest, sleeves cut off at the shoulder so that every inch of his powerful arms were on display.

Could a woman look at that and not wonder what it would be like to be held by him? Only if she wasn't human!

He had a white towel strung around his neck and his hair was dark with sweat, curling at the tips even though it was so short.

His facial features, she decided, were nauseatingly perfect. High cheekbones, straight, strong nose, faintly jutting chin. He hadn't shaved yet today, and for some reason that only made him look better, faintly roguish, untamable.

She knew all about this kind of man. They could have anything, and they took it. And when they were done they threw it back.

Only one thing stopped her from hating him completely—the look of muted panic that was in those amazing dark eyes as he surveyed her daughter.

"What does this kid eat? We're about out of options, here." He snapped this at her, like a military man on a mission that was about to fail.

Abby dragged her gaze away from him. Belle was settled happily on top of a stack of books on a chair, at a kitchen table covered with cereal boxes and bowls.

"You mean she's sampling everything?" Abby asked, aghast.

Her daughter took a regal bite of the offering in front of her, which looked like chocolate covered raisins in milk, swallowed, frowned and pointed autocratically at her next choice.

Which he, heartthrob of the universe, rushed to get for her.

"What are you doing?" Abby said, folding her arms across her chest. As if that would protect her. *From what?*

Her desire to laugh that's what, she told herself firmly. At the sight of one hundred and ninety pounds of one hundred percent menacing, masculine ex-cop being commanded by a baby.

"I'm feeding the kid." He glowered at Abby.

"Why?"

"When I came in from my run, she was just coming out the door of your suite. I tried to stuff her back in, but she wasn't having any of it. She announced she was hungry, and she damn well expected me to do something about it."

"In those words?" Abby couldn't resist teasing him.

"She doesn't need words! All she needs to do is screw up her face and show me her tonsils! When I told her to go back to Mommy, she yelled at me. Loudly."

"Belle!"

"Not a bad girl," Belle said, anticipating what was coming. "Belle bad?" she asked Shane and blinked at him with sweet coyness.

"Yes!" he said, but when Belle blinked again, he said, "Maybe not bad. Just stubborn, strong-willed, loud and fussy."

"She is not fussy," Abby addressed the only accusation that was not totally accurate. "She's taking advantage of you."

"A two-year-old?" He paused in his pouring of yet another sample into a bowl and drew himself to his full height, which was formidable, at least six feet, and gave Abby a disdainful look. "That seems unlikely."

"Really, you didn't have to feed her. You could have come and got me up."

"I thought of that." He added milk to the bowl, paused thoughtfully, and then added a sprinkle of brown sugar.

"And?" she asked, watching as he pondered for another moment, then dropped another dish of sugar on the cereal.

"You looked done in last night. I thought maybe you needed to sleep. Also, given that I promised you a secure room, I didn't think you'd appreciate waking up with a strange man hovering over you."

The very thought made her mouth go dry, actually. Did he have to be so devastatingly attractive?

Suddenly an uncomfortable reminder of what she must look like shot through her. Her hand flew to her hair. She could feel it standing straight up, and not in those cute little spikes she could accomplish with a tub of gel and a lot of patience. She glanced down at the rumpled clothes she had slept in. The buttons were done up crookedly on her blouse.

Naturally, he looked like he was ready for a photoshoot, even with the shadowed face, and sweat forming dark stains on his sweatshirt.

"One black shin is enough," he told her, with a sidelong look from under sooty, tangled lashes.

Abby looked at the leg she had kicked last night. It was sporting a rather large purple and blue bruise. Somehow, she doubted a kick would have been the first thought that would have come to her mind if Shane McCall had been the first thing she saw this morning.

"I hope that doesn't hurt too much." She thought she sounded very stiff, a woman transparently anxious to let a man know she could not be swayed by him, no matter how devastatingly attractive he was.

"To an old warrior?" he growled, then sighed. "Yeah, you bet it hurts."

"Mommy kiss better," Belle suggested wisely.

"Okay by me. What's Mommy have to say?" He said it casually, a man who knew the lines, but there was no emotion attached to the words, not even friendly teasing.

She kept her own features carefully bland. "Mommy's kisses are reserved for Belle. Only."

"That makes me feel real sorry for Belle's daddy," he said.

"A man less in need of your pity, you will never meet," she shot back, and then was sorry for all that she had revealed about herself with that one line. "Belle and I are on our own."

Still something about being in the same room with this scantily clothed man, and that word *kiss* hanging in the air between them, made the most bizarre thought crowd into her head.

I'm looking for a husband.

Her sister, Brittany, had said she was going to place an ad in the newspaper with similar wording after the three sisters had heard about the conditions placed on their gifts. And then Brittany had laughed with devil-may-care ease when Jordan Hamilton had treated her to a look of formidable disapproval.

But Abby wasn't Brittany. Not even if they did look identical.

"I think we've intruded quite enough," she said, the stiffness still in her voice. "We can be on our way now." *Before I make a complete fool of myself, not for the first time.*

Really, she had thrown herself at Ty, Belle's father, bowled over by his good looks and his easy charm, thinking they meant something. No man had ever made such a fuss over her before.

Besides, Ty's attentions had meant something. He wanted something. And as soon as he'd gotten it, the chase was over. Still, pregnant and afraid of being alone, she had stayed with him longer than any woman with an ounce of self-respect should have. He claimed, right up until the end, to love her madly, but still no offer of marriage had been forthcoming.

"I'll have a look at your car," Shane said.

Anybody, she reminded herself, could be charming. Anybody could seem like someone he was not.

"No," she said, watching as he stood there, carefully monitoring Belle's reaction to his latest offering. "That's unnecessary."

Brit would not approve. After all, hadn't she sent Abby that ridiculous book, *How to Find the Perfect Mate?* Abby had vowed not to read it, but found herself reading it anyway, with a kind of horrified fascination.

Had Brit sent one to Corrine as well? Corrine seemed a little clumsy in the man department, just like Abby.

Or maybe clumsy wasn't the right word. Corrine was more—aloof wasn't quite the right word. Reserved?

More like scared, Abby thought, wondering if only a sister would see behind the barriers in Corrine's eyes. Even a sister who had never known her. Well, who could blame her if she was scared? They were being asked, the three of them, to leave everything they had ever known and start over. With only each other.

It still shocked Abby that somebody who looked exactly like her could act like Brit.

Outgoing, bubbly, confident. Brit moved and talked and acted as if she believed she was incredibly beautiful.

And how could Abby look at her sister and see how beautiful she really was, and then look in the mirror and not see it at all in herself? Maybe, she should try her hair like Brit's—grow it out, let those curls go wild. A little more makeup, a little more style—but for what?

To attract that perfect man? she asked herself scornfully.

Abby bet Brit had sent Corrine a copy of that dreadful book, too. The book which had a whole chapter devoted to man-trapping grooming and dressing techniques.

And said absolutely nothing about what to do with wild, sticking-straight-up hair, and a morning-after look that was notably missing the night before. What use was a book that didn't deal with emergency situations?

Unless she just hadn't gotten to that chapter yet.

Abby, she reminded herself, *you hate that book and everything it stands for.*

Her mission was not to attract this man in front of her, even if he was just about as close to a perfect male specimen as she could probably hope to find in this lifetime, but to get away from him, leave him to his own life, and to find her own.

She could afford a mechanic, she reminded herself. Her meager savings were soon to be supplemented, because she had been given a house like this one, divided into two suites.

And her upstairs suite was inhabited by a reliable tenant. He'd been on the premises for nearly a year, and showed no signs of leaving, according to information she had from the management company.

With the income from him, and if she could pick up a bit of sewing, she and Belle would be just fine. Rich, by her standards.

Rich enough to have someone else come look at her car.

"I'll just call a service station," she said. "We've put you out enough."

"That now," Belle crowed, having rejected what was in the bowl in front of her.

"To be honest," he said, in a stage whisper "I think I'd rather look after the car than her."

"You don't have to do either. I'll take her out for breakfast. We don't need to trouble you any—"

"Nooo," Belle wailed. "Me like here."

"I guess, you would, you little minx. Don't you dare push that away! You love Sugar Pups!"

"Don't," Belle said mutinously.

And while Abby tried to do the impossible, reason with someone who had not yet fully developed reasoning skills, Shane picked her keys up from where she had left them on the table the night before and went out the door, whistling, one of those aggravating men who took control of everything.

Her feminist heart was appalled of course.

But her human one admitted wanting nothing more than to be looked after every now and then.

He felt, as he went down the walk, as though he had been hit over the head with a sack of bricks.

First, twenty pounds of tiny female wrapping him

around her little pink finger with complete ease, and then her mother coming in to finish the job.

How on earth could a woman look that good first thing in the morning?

Her hair going every which way, her blouse with the buttons done up crooked, her jeans all rumpled and so ridiculously large they were ready to fall off.

And she looked like a damned beauty queen.

Like with a flick of her finger, she could have had him pouring cereal for her, too.

He recognized this feeling as one he did not like and would not tolerate.

Shane McCall would not be vulnerable. Isn't that why he was here? In a little town where he didn't know a soul, and planned to keep it that way?

Correction: didn't know any girl souls.

He'd known Morgan for years, from when they had worked together on a temporary assignment on a drug smuggling case in Portland. Morgan had moved back here, to his hometown of Miracle Harbor, to get married and have babies. Morgan had invited him to come for dinner one night. Meet his wife, his kids.

The wife he might have been able to handle, but kids?

He couldn't be around kids.

He didn't want to *feel* things. Guys talked about basketball scores and work. Kids related on a different level entirely. And women, well, he wasn't even going to go there.

An old pal on the Drug Unit, Drew Duarte worried about him, had pulled him back from a life of complete loneliness and despair by begging him to help out with training. So he did specialized training sessions a few times a year, which is why he ran and lifted weights. He wasn't letting any young buck ten years his junior run him into the ground. Now, Drew had him taking it a step further. He was working on a chapter on drug detection procedures for a Federal enforcement agency training manual.

Maybe a life where the thing a man was most grateful for was the spelling checker on his computer had gotten a little too controlled, even for him.

Had he wished for something else, even for a moment? Yearned?

No!

Maybe moving to a place called Miracle Harbor was asking for trouble. Which, he told himself, with annoyance, was not a rational thought at all.

It was the thought of a man whose calm and orderly life had been disrupted.

He'd moved here because he had to get away from where he was. Leave it behind him. Morgan had sent a sympathy card when he'd heard, and there had been a note tucked inside, saying if Shane needed a place to get away for a while, his family had a cottage on the ocean.

He'd come, planning to stay a week, and somehow never left.

He'd moved from Morgan's drafty cottage after his first winter, and rented both suites of this old Dutch Colonial house, ideally located a block from downtown and the ocean. It was too big for a single guy, but he didn't want any of the neighborly intimacy of sharing a house. Rentals in Miracle Harbor were nearly impossible to come by at anytime, and the situation had worsened with the resort project going up on the outside of town. The house was ancient and somewhat like a cranky old lady, constantly demanding. The furnace was finicky, the windows didn't open, the lights flickered, and he seemed to look forward to each catastrophe with the relish of a person who didn't have enough in his life to care about. The house suited him perfectly.

So, he'd fix the little problem that had come into his neat and tidy life with the same calm determination that he fixed the problems that came up with the old house. In no time, he would be rid of the disrupting pair of little-her, and big-her. Really, he was killing two birds with one stone—doing the Boy Scout thing, something he was reluctantly aware of missing now that he no longer had active duty, and getting rid of them at the same time.

"Win-win, I would say," he muttered to himself.

He opened her car door and slid in, reaching down to pop the hood. There was a book peeking out of a pocket of a travel bag that sat on the front seat. It felt like the title was blinking on and off like a neon sign.

He actually felt the sweat pop out on his brow as he read it.

How to Find the Perfect Mate.

Well, hadn't he known that was what she was looking for from the first moment she had turned those huge, vulnerable eyes on him?

This woman needed a man.

And it sure as hell wasn't going to be him.

It gave him added incentive to get the car going, which he did in very short order.

Whistling, wiping grease from his hands, he went back into his house.

She was on the phone. The baby was playing on the floor with his plastic bowls, but other than that, the kitchen was immaculate. All the cereal had been put away and the bowls were washed and stored. The baby made a beeline for him, grinning from ear to ear.

Was it that easy to make friends with a baby? *Beware the warm feeling in your chest, Shane McCall.* He sidled away from Belle, who lunged after him, undeterred.

He was on this third loop around the kitchen table when Abby hung up the phone and gave him a worried look. "The law office doesn't seem to be open on Saturday. I tried Jordan Hamilton, the lawyer looking after our case, at home, but there was no answer."

"One of his sons practices with him. Mitch." Mitch Hamilton was a friend of Morgan's. "I'll call him." But when he looked for the number in the book, it wasn't there. He called Morgan.

The baby Belle was hugging his knee. He shook his leg slightly. She held on a little tighter. He could hear a kid laughing in the background on Morgan's end. The one holding on to his leg was making little squawking noises, too.

"I bought the kids a dog," his friend told him after Shane greeted him and asked him for Mitch's number.

"I can tell from the noise level that was a big hit."

"It was stupid thing to do," Morgan confided in a low tone. " I've been cleaning up dog poop for six days."

Shane listened to the kids laughing in the background and felt that swell of feeling inside himself. He wasn't quite sure what it was, some form of grief for joys he would not know, but he pushed it back, and reached down and pried the chubby fingers off his knee. Her mother got the hint and came and took her. "That number?"

Mitch Hamilton answered on the second ring, listened to the problem. Shane heard only blessed silence in the background. No little kids running around that house.

"Dad's away on business this weekend," Mitch told him. "I'll run into the office. I was going in anyway."

Good man, Shane thought, going to the office on Saturday, not cleaning up dog poop in a house filled to the rafters with laughter.

"Thanks."

"I'll double-check the address of her house, and call you back. What did she think the address was again? Twenty-two Harbor? And which triplet is she?"

"Abby."

"Does she have long hair?"

What did that have to do with anything? "Nope."

"Okay." Did he sound relieved? "I'll call you within the hour."

Fifteen minutes would have been better, but Shane knew he was in no position to complain.

"It's going to take him about an hour," he said. He noticed her buttons were done up straight now, and her hair had been sternly flattened. He'd liked it better wild. "Have you eaten yet?"

"No."

The kid was back on the floor, tottering around, her arms straight out from her shoulders like airplane wings. She was laughing at nothing, not even a puppy, that sweet laughter filling up his house, a house that had been blissfully empty until now. Blissfully.

"Help yourself to breakfast," he said curtly. "I've got a ton of cereal. And a ton of work to do. I'll just head up to my office until we hear from Mitch."

"Sure. Thanks. Fine."

"And one other thing, Abby?"

"Yes?"

I'm not the perfect mate. Not even close. But somehow he couldn't bring himself to say it. "The coffeemaker is over there, if you feel like some. Just make yourself at home.''

As soon as he said those words he felt an odd shiver go up and down his spine.

He went upstairs, listening to her talk to Belle, then hit the shower. When he came out, the smell of coffee had drifted up the stairs. He *wanted* the coffee, but he *needed* to avoid fraternizing with the invading army. He forced himself to sit down at his computer and turn it on. In the next hour, he wrote two lines, neither of which made much sense when he read them over.

When the phone finally rang, he picked it up with all the desperation of a drowning man reaching for a life preserver.

Only the life preserver turned out to be something else entirely.

Once he hung up the phone he went back down the stairs, stood in the kitchen doorway watching them. Big-her was sitting on the kitchen floor blowing soap bubbles for little-her.

''Was that the lawyer?'' she asked over her shoulder.

He nodded, dumbly, like a man who had stood too close to a bomb going off and was still reeling from the shock.

She got up off the floor and wiped slippery hands on her jeans. ''Did he find my house?''

''That's the good news.'' He could smell fresh coffee and avoiding the question in her eyes, he walked over and took some, keeping his back carefully to her.

''Oh-oh. That means there's bad news. Doesn't it?''

He glanced over his shoulder, saw anxiety knit her brow, and swiftly returned to stirring his coffee. Why would he want to wipe that anxious look off her face?

As it turned out, he was the one with the problem, the one with things to be anxious about.

His idea that she was leaving soon, nice-meeting-you-have-a-nice-life leaving, had just been blasted to smithereens by that lawyer.

Who had assured him, no mistake. He'd double-checked it.

Out of the corner of his eye, Shane watched his silence make her shoulders slump, so he turned and faced her, took a long sip of his coffee and cleared his throat.

"Just tell me," she said, bravely, jamming her hands into her blue jean pockets. "I should have known. It's probably falling down, right? A wreck. I won't be able to live in it."

"That's not exactly the problem, no."

"The tenant is awful?" she guessed. "He's a filthy old man. He's living in *my* house with three goats and sixteen tomcats, isn't he?"

"No."

"Tell me," she implored. "Please."

"Miss Blakely, it would seem *this* is your house."

Chapter Three

"This is *my* house?" Abby said.

"Yeah," Shane said. He didn't miss the way she was looking around with a brand-new kind of interest, seeing the potential for a picture here and a splash of paint there, planning where she was going to put her rocking chair.

There was even a word for the look in her eyes.

Nesting. He knew, because he'd been through it all before. Stacey, when they had bought that falling-down house, had had those stars in her eyes, seeing a castle instead of a catastrophe. Shane was pretty sure he could not survive *that* again.

Of course, he wasn't married to this woman. And she wasn't going to die. Hopefully. Hopefully, she was going to accept, with good grace, that there had been a terrible mix-up, and that *her* house was already inhabited by a most reliable tenant.

Who, according to her lawyer, did not have a legal leg to stand on once his lease expired, in two months.

He looked at her face. And didn't feel very hopeful.

"It's so beautiful," she breathed. "Look at the floors."

Shane glared at her. "They need to be refinished. Your baby will be getting slivers from them. The furnace doesn't work properly. The doors and windows don't open or shut the way they should. Drafts. Drafts are very bad for babies."

In his own ears, he sounded like exactly what he was—a desperate man.

"Somehow you don't strike me as any kind of expert on babies," she said, not at all concerned, running her hands lightly and lovingly over the stained oak window casing and sill.

"I could refinish this."

For an insane moment he thought he would like to tell her that he had almost become an expert on babies, once, a long time ago. There was something in her eyes that said she would know what to do with that information, would know exactly what to do.

That this renegade thought would slip so easily past the carefully constructed wall of his control, shocked him, though shock was not the exact word that described how he felt. He ordered his mind not to replace shocked with the truth: scared.

"The whole electrical system probably needs to be replaced!" he said, instead. "Not to mention the outside stairs. For starters."

"Have you noticed many spiders?" she asked him.

"Spiders?"

"Yes."

"I can't say I've noticed any spiders."

"Oh, well, then, everything else sounds like small

problems,'' she said airily, dismissing them with a wave of her hand.

That was a woman for you. Major structural problems dismissed. But a spider, that was something else. He suspected if he'd told her the place was overrun with spiders, she'd be gone in a blink. But he didn't have that kind of dishonesty in him. He hoped to get rid of her fair and square.

''You seem to be forgetting one quite large problem,'' he said, his voice stern and unyielding in an effort to claim her undivided attention and to convince himself his control was not slipping.

''I'm going to paper the front hallway with a pattern that has yellow teacup roses in it,'' she said dreamily. ''And get a handwoven Finnish throw rug for the front door. And I'll make red-checked curtains for this window in here. What do you think of red checks?''

''We were discussing the problem,'' he reminded her. He thought red checks would be awful, give the kitchen the ambience of an Italian restaurant.

''Oh, sorry, what problem is that?''

''Me.'' He folded his arms across his chest. As an ex-cop he knew all about practicing *presence,* making himself seem bigger and more intimidating than he was. And at just a hair over six feet he was already plenty big and somewhat intimidating.

She didn't seem the least bit concerned. She was looking thoughtfully at the moldings, even got down on her haunches and ran her fingertips along one. She smiled. ''Real oak.''

''Me?'' he reminded her.

She stood up, regarded him thoughtfully, then smiled. The light in her eyes was damned near blinding.

"It looks like you're an excellent tenant. I think we could work things out."

"Really?" he said uneasily. Somehow he did not think her solution was going to involve simply dropping by once a month to pick up her rent check like a good little landlady.

"Why couldn't we share the place?" she asked. "That would save you having to find a new place to live, and it would save me from having to find a new tenant."

"Aren't you just little Miss Reasonable?" he said.

"I think I'm being very reasonable."

Really, he thought, there was nothing unreasonable about her suggestion, except that it put him under the same roof as her. And little-her. Which was completely unacceptable.

"Shane," she said, her voice soft, her eyes huge on his face, "I don't have anywhere else to go."

She wasn't going to pull that woman-in-trouble stuff on him. She'd already worked that once, and look where it had gotten him.

"Last night," he reminded her coldly, "You didn't even want to come in. Now you want to live here?"

"Now I know it's mine," she said.

"Women's logic has always failed me," he said. He'd known her less than one full day, and already his life was in tatters. Disrupted. His familiar routines threatened.

"Do you have anywhere else to go?" she asked him.

He opened his mouth. He wanted to say he had dozens of places he could go. Dozens. But instead, the truth slipped out. "No." He hastily added, "But I could buy a place."

He didn't tell her the part of that equation that made

it unworkable. Buying a house involved a little thing called commitment, a word he had carefully and totally eradicated from his vocabulary.

"But I've already invested quite a bit in this one," he stubbornly said, instead.

"I know we can work this out."

Shane didn't want to work anything *out*. The only context in which he wanted the word out used was toward her—as in out of his hair, out of his house.

Except that it was her house.

He noticed she took over his coffeepot, refilling the mug he had already nearly drained.

"The countertops need a little work," she said.

"The house needs a little work," he said, "and I use the term 'little' loosely. Ten carpenters employed full time for a month—and good luck finding even one in this town for the next year or two—couldn't make a dent in all the things wrong with this place."

"I could trade you. Reduced rent for doing some of the work." She helped herself to a coffee and went and sat down at the table, looking around with plans in her eyes. A countertop here, a cupboard door there.

His life being mapped out for him.

Why hadn't the lawyer come over? He was probably an expert at dealing with these kinds of complicated situations that arose with such frequency when men and women tried to share lives. But most of them had *agreed* to share their lives.

Shane pulled out a chair, and sat down uneasily across from her. He had no sooner taken a sip of his coffee, when he felt a familiar little hand on his knee. Belle, having abandoned the plastic bowls, pulled herself up and stared expectantly at him. He stared back.

"Up?" she asked.

"No." She looked cute as could be. Her mother had dressed her in little red overalls, and had tamed the unruly blond curls into a funny little ponytail at the top of the baby's head. But the thing was if you gave an inch to any member of the female species, the next thing you knew—

"Pwease?"

—your heart was broken. It was not the thought he had intended to have. At all. He stared hard at little Belle, glanced at Abby, and then gave in with ill grace. How the hell did you say no to a baby? He reached down and put the little girl on his lap. Oblivious to his mood, apparently not anymore intimidated by *presence* than her mother, she sighed happily, rested her head against his chest, put her thumb in his mouth.

Still, despite their immunity to his *presence,* the cop in him kicked in. Find out the whole story, and then the solution might be more obvious.

"So," he said, "How did you come to be in possession of this house?"

The whole story was that she was an orphan who had only just recently learned she was one of triplets. She and each of her sisters had been given a gift, by a stranger, that reunited them here in Miracle Harbor.

This house was her gift.

A lot of his questions were answered, but instead of feeling clear, he felt more muddled. First of all the policeman in him did not like it one little bit that a stranger, a person she knew nothing about, had given her a house.

Secondly, hearing her story made Abby Blakely not just an irritating problem who had presented herself on his doorstep, but a human being, three-dimensional, with her own history and feelings. Not the enemy. And if he wasn't careful, all those things were going to work against him. The baby on his lap was part of the same plot.

Shane tried to steel himself. Her tragedy-filled life was not his concern. Still, he had to ask. "How come you and your sisters were split up, anyway?"

She shrugged, but not before he caught a glimpse of intense pain in her eyes. "I'm just starting to get parts of the story now. My sister Brittany says she was adopted when she was about three by her parents. My sister Corrine said her parents were killed in a car accident. So, I'm assuming my parents were killed in a car accident when I was about three, and for some awful reason we were split up. Still, my life is like a puzzle that I don't have all the pieces to. I think as I get to know my sisters, more and more will fall into place. And maybe whoever gave me this house knows something."

Her voice cracked just a little bit, before she composed herself and bravely went on. "The only way I'll ever find out is if I stay here, give this a chance."

"The suites in this house don't even have separate kitchens!" Shane pointed, trying to use practicality in the face of emotion, a ploy he knew would not work. She was just another human being, doing her best with the cards that had been given her, a hand nearly as good as his own.

Still, he saw no self-pity in her, but great courage, a hint of pure steel. Which probably did not bode well for his future living arrangements.

"I do have a lease," Shane pointed out.

"For how long?" she whispered.

"Not for long enough to have any bearing on this

conversation, unfortunately,'' he admitted, slightly ashamed of himself for the anxiety he had caused to appear in her face.

Geez. What was he doing? For him it was a house. A place to live. He had no attachment to it.

She apparently, had hopes and dreams wrapped up in this house. Already.

Belle picked that moment to reach up and insert a finger in his nose, reminding him that Abby's interests probably were a little more pressing than his. Still, he felt the last of his hardline stance evaporating.

He could probably find another place to live if he gave his life over to finding it. Which he discovered he was prepared to do. He wasn't going to live under the same roof as her, indefinitely.

"You can't live with your sisters?" he asked, one desperate, last-ditch effort.

He removed Belle's finger, looked at her face, and sighed.

She wasn't going to live with her sisters.

"You see, Shane," she said softly, "I need to live in this house. I can't really explain it. But it has to do with the fact that somebody cared enough about me that they gave me this place. This house is mine, the first thing that's ever been mine. Besides Belle. Can you understand that?"

"Not really," he said gruffly. Her answer showed him another huge chasm between male and female perception. Or maybe it was cop and civilian perception. Whatever it was, he saw her receiving the house as a gift as somewhat suspicious. She saw it in an entirely different light, like the universe was pouring love on her. He sighed heavily.

"I'll go. As soon as I find a place. That might take a while in this town."

"You don't have to go."

"Yes," he said firmly, feeling the sweet weight of the baby in his lap, "I do."

He wondered, right away, how on earth she was going to get a tenant as good as him. Not his problem, he told himself firmly.

Belle bounced on his lap and sang a little song, that seemed to consist of the words "no-go-away-today."

"You don't have to go," Abby said again. "Shane, you don't even use this ground floor suite. You told me that last night. There's plenty of room down here for Belle and I. And there's no reason we couldn't share the kitchen."

"That doesn't work for me," he said.

"Now I feel guilty."

So was he supposed to feel guilty that she felt guilty? Damn, life became complicated with a woman involved. He bet himself he could have a new place to live within a week, if he really worked at it.

And what if she rented the suite to an old man with sixteen tomcats and a goat?

Not his problem.

Even if she did have to share the kitchen with him.

"I'll haul your stuff in." There. "You might as well stay here until I've found a new place. I guess we can share the kitchen until then."

She'd managed to make him feel guilty, anyway. He'd just had his house pulled right out from under him, and *he* felt guilty.

And that's what women did. Turned your world upside down and topsy-turvy before you knew what was happening.

If he *really* worked at it, and wasn't too fussy, he bet he could have himself a new place to live in three days.

"Belle," Abby whispered to her daughter, gathering her in her arms and waltzing around the empty kitchen, after Shane had left. "This is our house! Ours! Yours and mine!"

"And man's?" Belle asked, smiling at her mother's happiness, touching her cheek.

"Oh, him. I don't know about him, Belle." The truth was she felt guilty. Why should she feel guilty? He was the stubborn one!

"Me like," Belle announced.

"Only because of what he gave you for breakfast. You shouldn't allow yourself to be so easily bought. A life lesson from your mother."

Belle smiled with absolutely no understanding.

Abby set her down on the floor, and surveyed the room. It needed everything. New countertops. New cabinets. New flooring.

But for now, new curtains, and a coat of paint would make it hers. And, of course, curtains were one of her specialities. And maybe he was right. Maybe she'd better be careful just how attached she became to the place. Because if she wasn't married in a year, it wouldn't be hers.

She decided she wasn't even going to think about that right now. Right now she was going to count her blessings. She didn't even have to worry about that car. Let it sit there! She could walk to downtown from here. And to the beach.

"Abby!"

She recognized his voice, and the annoyance in it. She already knew a few things about Shane McCall. She could tell by the way he lined things up in his cupboards with military precision and from the fact that there was not a speck of dirt anywhere, that he was a man who liked control.

Loved control.

She thought it was a measure of the kind of man he really was, and not the kind he wanted her to think he was, that he had accepted this unexpected loss of his control with a kind of reluctant grace.

Probably just what he needed, the old sourpuss. When he saw how quietly she and Belle lived, he might not move after all. She didn't want to be looking for a new tenant in a town full of transient workers.

"Abby!"

Of course, she was not at all sure she would be able to handle living with him either. Maybe, she thought whimsically, she'd just let the universe look after it.

It was not doing a bad job so far.

Tucking Belle under her arm, she went out of the kitchen.

Shane McCall was standing in her front hallway, dressed about the same as he had been last night—in next to nothing. Shorts. She could see his shirt hanging from a rhododendron in the yard.

Her eyes took in the bulge of muscle in Shane's arms as he carried her sewing machine. Her glance trailed to the column of his throat, the little trickle of sweat that chased down from behind his ear.

"Where would you like me to put this?" he asked.

She knew where he wanted to put it, right out the door, back on the trailer and out of his life.

"Over by the window would be very nice."

"What is it, anyway?" he panted. "Bricks in a box?"

"My serger."

"What?"

"It's a kind of sewing machine."

Just as she said it, the handle on the carrying case, wobbly for some time, groaned and tore away. He caught the box before it hit the ground, but it glanced off his toe.

He said three words in a row she was not sure she had ever heard before. She set her daughter down. "Belle, go play with those bowls in the kitchen. Shane, really, I don't want my daughter learning that kind of language."

He looked sorry and stubborn at the same time. He glared at her. "It's just as well that you don't get any ideas," he said.

"About what?"

"About taming me."

"About taming you?" she echoed.

"I'm leaving. Soon. And I am not the perfect man."

She eyed him suspiciously. Was it coincidental that he had picked that phrase? It must be. She hadn't brought in that book. Would the lawyer he spoke to on the phone have revealed to him the condition placed on receiving the gift? Warned Shane she was on the hunt for a husband, just like her sisters?

"I don't think you're in any danger of being mistaken for a perfect man."

Now he looked insulted.

"Mostly," she added hastily, "because in my experience, there is no such thing."

"I'm going to start to look for another place to live this afternoon."

"Suit yourself."

"I will," he muttered.

"Though I must admit, I'd feel very safe at night if you were to stay."

He snorted.

"But good luck finding another place," she said cheerfully. "You know what? I love this room. Look at the light. I can have my plants over there, and still have room to have my mannequin here."

"Your mannequin," he said flatly, shoving the sofa against the wall and turning to look at her.

"I'm a seamstress. I plan to hang out my shingle."

"Soon?"

"As soon as possible."

"I can't have a whole lot of noise and commotion while I'm working," he told her. He had folded his arms over his chest again, and planted his legs far apart.

Really, it made him look ten feet tall and bulletproof. They'd probably taught him how to look like that in policeman school. If she ever let him think he'd intimidated her, she'd be lost, and she knew it.

"Shane, do you know anything about sewing?"

"Not really."

"It's not exactly loud. Much of what I do, like hemming, and beading, is by hand. My sewing machine, when I use it, is ultraquiet. I tried out quite a few of them before I found one a baby could sleep through."

"But people coming here? Knocking on the door at all hours of the day and night?"

"I'm going to take in a little sewing, not be running a bootlegging operation. I'm sure you'll find it won't disturb you at all before you go. You won't even know we're here, Belle and I."

"And are you willing to put that in writing?"

Before she could reply there was a loud crash from the kitchen and a wail from Belle. She hurried away, but not before she noticed him roll his eyes, and heard him mutter, "Gee, I barely know you're here, already."

Chapter Four

"**I** can't hear you," Shane said into the phone. "It's what? Board and room? That's not what the ad says...reduced rent for what? Can you turn down that noise? I can barely hear you. You can't turn down your kids? Reduced rent for *baby-sitting?*"

He slammed down the phone, without saying good-bye, and put a vicious pen slash through the second-to-last For Rent ad in the morning edition of the *Miracle Harbor Beacon*.

Downstairs, he heard her. Singing again. Obviously when this old dump had been renovated not a single thought had been given to soundproofing. And she had been singing as if her heart were overflowing with joy since he had hauled in the last of her things around seven o'clock last night. He'd heard her unpacking her newly purchased groceries in the kitchen.

If it had been rock and roll, he could have told her to can it.

But she didn't sing rock and roll. She sang ballads, loaded with haunting Celtic lilt.

Even worse than the singing was what he heard once it had grown quiet in her apartment last night, the kid apparently finally asleep in a crib that had been more complicated to assemble than a Chinese puzzle. Just when he had thought his life was going to be returned to blessed silence, he had heard the water going into the downstairs tub. Her tub. And then he had heard what he had to presume was her filling her tub.

He resented the fact that in just a little more than twenty-four hours his whole life had been wrested out of his control. To be honest, he was weary of fate throwing wrenches into the well-oiled machinery of his life.

She splashed and sighed and hummed in that bathtub for long enough that he had to go out for a good brisk walk. He'd succeeded in completely clearing his mind of her, too. Put together in his mind six or seven pretty good paragraphs on proper stakeout technique.

But then he'd made the mistake of coming back through the lane, and had seen the candlelight flickering through the frosted panes of her bathroom window.

A disturbing mental picture had formed. Of her. In that bathtub. Wearing only bubbles. With the candle flame dancing and throwing erotic shadows on the wall.

His body's reaction had been instant, embarrassing in a man his age. Going up the stairs to his suite, two steps at a time, he couldn't help but wonder if his monkish lifestyle was making him into the pervert she'd accused him of being.

What was wrong with him? Adolescent boys pictured women naked. He didn't. Wouldn't. To prove it he had proceeded to throw himself into his work with single-minded fury. At midnight, when he had not heard a sound in her quarters for the better part of an hour, he reviewed what he had just spent three hours working on.

He was shocked to find that he had written sixteen paragraphs of drug-bust gibberish. He'd turned off the computer without saving, gone to bed, and had lain awake.

An hour later, he'd crept down the stairs into the kitchen, a man bent on a bologna sandwich.

His bologna, only two weeks old, had been disposed of. So had an open can of sardines.

His fridge was jam-packed with green things. Lettuce. Broccoli. Asparagus. Way in the back, behind 2% milk and smoked Gouda, he found a can of soda that he knew was his.

He debated trying the Gouda, but decided what his life was going to need, if he was going to survive the next few days, were rules.

Starting with thou shalt not touch the other guy's Gouda. Or bologna, as the case might be.

Still unable to sleep, he'd returned to his section of the house, and begun a list of rules and a schedule for kitchen use. When dawn broke, he went for a run and got a newspaper.

He hadn't prayed for a long, long time, but he sent a little plea heavenward as he dialed the last number in the For Rent section of the classified ads.

Yes, it was a house. No, no, not for sharing. Perfect for a single man.

He began to get suspicious. In his experience, no one *wanted* to rent to a single guy. At least not until they met him.

Small, but clean, he was assured.

The address? That nice little row of cottages on Cannery Street.

He hung up the phone, no goodbye again. There were no cottages on Cannery Street. There were shacks. Depressing places with Rottweilers chained in the front yards, and cars decomposing in the back. All the houses had an impressive view of the old Jones' Brothers Cannery, closed for at least fifteen years, rotting away at the end of a tilting dock. It was the part of town that nobody in Miracle Harbor wanted to admit was there.

Displeased with the results of his house hunting, he allowed himself to review his kitchen schedule with a flicker of satisfaction. He would take early shift in the morning, before she was even up. And then it would be his again at twelve-thirty. He only needed a few minutes to make lunch. He could have supper late, between seven and eight. An electric kettle should look after the odd urge for a cup of coffee.

The schedule actually might be workable, he thought. The way he had things planned, it was possible he would never lay eyes on her. No more sessions with a baby on his lap. A thing like that could muddle a man's thinking.

He had his own bathroom, so really they were sharing a kitchen and a hallway. Maybe that wouldn't inconvenience him nearly as much as he thought it would.

Her voice, full of merriment, floated up through the cracks in the floor, and the pipes, and the hollow walls.

"The bear went over the mountain, the bear went over the mountain, the bear went over the mountain, to seeee what he could seeeeee."

Little-her cracked up, shouting with laughter.

Savagely, he crossed out the last ad, and retrieved his phone book. At the back was a listing of apartments, and even though he had sworn he would never again live in an apartment building, he began the tedious job of calling them about vacancies.

After an hour, he'd had about enough of hearing people snort at him when he asked about vacancies. Underneath, Do Not Remove Other People's Belongings from the Fridge, he scrawled, No Singing, then recognized that in pursuit of his own survival he was becoming churlish, and crossed it off. His stay here was only temporary. What did it matter if she sang?

The doorbell rang.

He frowned, not sure he had heard the doorbell before. He waited for her to get it, but heard only silence. The doorbell rang again. And then again.

She hadn't even been here a full day. What were the chances that it was for her?

He'd been in Miracle Harbor for two years, and there was even less chance it was for him. He liked what that said about his life. He'd succeeded at removing himself from entanglements of any kind.

The doorbell rang again.

He'd be better at getting rid of a salesman than her, anyway.

He picked up his schedule, and his rules and bounded down the steps. At the last moment, too late, his mind registered the baby gate. Where there had been nothing before, now there was a wooden gate, two and a half feet high, at the bottom of the steps.

He tried to leap over it, but his toe caught and he crashed painfully to the floor, leading with his knee. It felt like the kneecap was shattered. He swore a blue streak, reached down and gingerly manipulated the knee. Not broken. He swore some more, remembered the baby, and satisfied himself with several low and heartfelt growls of pain mixed with aggravation.

The doorbell rang again.

He got painfully to his feet and limped over. Rubbing his knee, he swung open the door, and got ready to blast whoever stood there.

The blast died inside of him.

The sweetest little old lady stood outside his door, her gray hair in a prim bun, her lovely blue eyes, which had somehow remained young even as her face had aged, twinkling merrily at him. She was wearing a hat, with a jaunty red feather in it, and her hands were folded primly over a pocketbook. She looked exactly like the granny who loved Tweety-Bird so dearly.

He braced himself. It was going to be hard to slam the door in her face if she asked him if he'd been saved.

"Hello, dear," she said gently.

Dear. She'd heard him cussing a blue streak, and still called him dear? "Uh, hello."

"You don't look very much like a seamstress." She chuckled. "Is this where the seamstress lives?"

He was so relieved that she wasn't handing him a tract, that he stood and stared stupidly at her for a moment. "Seamstress? There's no—"

Then he remembered his toe, which was as black-and-blue as his shin and now his knee were, and the heavy object he had dropped on it. Some kind of a sewing machine. A seiger? That didn't sound exactly right, but it was in keeping with the fact his life was under siege. "Oh," he said. "*That* seamstress."

The door to the seamstress's apartment opened, and Abby came out, her cheeks flushed and her short hair curling wildly, a damp baby wrapped in a thick white towel in her arms.

It seemed to him a proper seamstress should look more like the little old lady at the door than like Abby. Abby was wearing jeans, three sizes too large, that rode down low on her hips. She had on some kind of sawed-off white top that was wet enough to hint at what was underneath it. Her belly button was showing.

Her belly button, and the secrets under that top both looked like they were even better than he had imagined last night.

"Did you fall?" Abby asked him, her eyes wide on his face. "I heard the most horrible crash."

In answer, he dragged his eyes away from her, and turned and glared at the baby gate.

"Oh, dear," she whispered. "I only put it up an hour ago. I didn't want Belle disturbing you. I thought you'd notice it."

"If I'd had a proper night's sleep I might have."

"A proper night's sleep? But I didn't disturb you, did I?"

"No!" he snapped, knowing a bald-faced lie could occasionally be concealed with uncalled-for aggression. The baby was humming about the damned bear, and he just knew when he tried to go to sleep tonight that tune would be caught in his head, and the bear would go over the mountain again and again and again.

Which was far preferable, really, to his thinking about Abby's wet shirt and belly button, or candles, wet skin and bubbles.

"Are you hurt?" she asked anxiously.

It would be easy to kill her tender concern. All he'd have to do is let her know what he was thinking. He could kill two birds with one stone. She'd probably pack her bags and be out of here in the blink of an eye. Pervert confirmed.

He told himself he didn't only out of deference to the baby, and the little old lady, who was looking back and forth between them with bird-like interest.

His knee was throbbing painfully. He could feel it swelling. "No." He nodded at the door. "You have a visitor."

"A visitor? But I don't know anyone here."

"I'm looking for a seamstress," the old lady said, helpfully.

"Really?" Abby said, delight lighting up her voice. "Come in."

Shane pushed open the screen and held it as the little old gal moved daintily by him. She rewarded him with a lovely smile.

"Thank you, dear. Just when I thought chivalry was dead."

"Yeah, well," he said, and then had a brainstorm. "You aren't in the market for an apartment are you? The one upstairs is for rent."

"Oh, I don't do stairs, dear. Besides, isn't that where you live?"

He frowned at her. How could she know that? She must have heard him coming down them. He muttered, "Not for very much longer, I don't."

Still, he wanted Abby to have a tenant just like this little old lady. Did any little old ladies do stairs? He sighed heavily. He supposed he was going to have to look after that, too. Finding Abby a tenant who wouldn't think evil thoughts every time he heard her bath running.

He turned and picked his kitchen schedule up off the floor.

"These are the hours I'll be in the kitchen. I'm posting a schedule on the fridge door."

Without waiting for her to reply, he went into the kitchen. Little magnets in the shapes of pears and peaches graced a fridge door that had always been plain white.

"How very handy," he said out loud, posting the rules with a little fuzzy peach.

The hallway was empty when he came back out, her door shut. He stepped over the gate, though the maneuver caused his leg to scream with pain, and went back up the stairs and back into his office. He shut the door with a little more force than was absolutely necessary, picked up a piece of blank paper from his desk, and wrote:

"Wanted—tenant for upstairs apartment. Shared kitchen and entryway." He thought about it for a moment, and squeezed the word reliable in between wanted and tenant. And then he squeezed the words female only between apartment and shared. He put down his own phone number, and dialed the *Beacon*.

Abby's visitor moved by her into her suite. She reached out and touched the baby's cheek with a gnarled hand.

"How nice that the young man is posting a schedule to let you know when he'll be in the kitchen," she said, looking at Abby over round wire-rimmed glasses. "He must want you to join him!"

"I don't think that is quite his intent," Abby muttered, noticing that even as she tried to focus on her visitor, her mind kept drifting back to the *nice* young man.

The look in his eyes when she'd come out the door hadn't been nice at all.

Not, she decided, that it had been angry either, which

is what she had expected when she had heard that awful crash. The look in his eyes had changed the color of them, made them even darker and more intense than they usually were. The look had been—what?

She became aware of an uncomfortable dampness down her front and glanced down at her shirt.

She flushed, recognizing exactly the look she had seen in his eyes.

Heat.

She gave herself a mental shake, that did nothing for the heat rising, suddenly and inexplicably, up her own neck. She freed one hand from underneath the towel and desperately tried to focus on her visitor.

"I'm Abby Blakely. How can I help you?"

"I'm Angela Pondergrove. For some silly reason people call me Angel. I'm looking for a seamstress. Imagine my surprise when *he* opened the door. It does seem a little early in the year for short pants, but I must say his legs made my heart race in a way it hasn't done for quite some time. Don't you think he has the nicest legs?"

Abby thought she had given the gorgeous legs of her tenant quite enough thought.

"How on earth did you hear about me being a seamstress?" she asked, instead of answering the question. "I just got here."

"Oh, Jordan said something to me," she said vaguely. "Jordan Hamilton. The lawyer?"

"That was nice of him, but I don't remember telling him I was a seamstress."

The old lady held out her frail arms. "May I hold the baby? You must have said something. Perhaps a chance remark. Jordan doesn't miss a thing, you know."

Abby hesitated before passing her Belle. For one thing, Mrs. Pondergrove looked frail, like the weight of stout little Belle might be too much for her. For another, Belle did not always take to strangers, not that it was obvious from her reaction to the man upstairs.

Come to think of him, she felt a certain unwanted *heat* when she looked at him, too. She thought maybe they should come up with a list of rules.

The first one being: Thou shalt keep all your clothes on.

Belle went willingly to Mrs. Pondergrove after all, and the old woman had quite a bit more strength in her arms than Abby would have thought.

"Come sit down," Abby suggested.

Mrs. Pondergrove did, and after making a fuss over Belle for a while longer, she set her between them on the couch and took a picture from the pocket of a gray wool jacket that, though tasteful, had seen better days.

"This is what I was wondering about," Mrs. Pondergrove said softly.

Abby took the picture, and drew in a startled breath. The picture was a line drawing of a wedding gown. It featured a high collar, and a sweetheart neckline shaped like a perfect teardrop. The effect was a dress that was innocent and sexy at the same time. The entire bodice was beautifully beaded and formfitting to the waist, where the skirt was attached in a sensuous vee that would accentuate the soft roundness of a woman's hips. Then the line of the gown fell in beautiful and breathtaking simplicity to the floor. A full train flowed out behind it.

"It's beautiful," she breathed. It was the kind of dress every girl dreamed of. Exactly the kind of dress she had once believed she would wear.

Before Ty. And Belle. And the death of her silly, Cinderella notions. So why, looking at this dress, could she suddenly see herself in it? And why did that picture cause an unexpected yearning, almost like pain, to rise up in her?

It was as if the dress shouted her best kept secret. That underneath all her proclamations of independence, underneath how competently she handled the challenges and rigors of being a single mother, there was this hope, still, that someday love would happen to her.

"Is something wrong?" Mrs. Pondergrove asked.

"Of course not, no," she said hastily, but put the picture down on the couch beside her all the same.

"Could you make that dress?" Mrs. Pondergrove asked her anxiously.

Abby looked again at the picture, without picking it up. Could she make that dress? Of course she could. It would be a dream to make such a dress. She could almost feel the richness of the fabric beneath her fingers, just from looking at the drawing. It would have to be silk. Nothing else would do the dress justice.

She could make the dress, but what of her own dreams? Wouldn't making such a dress make her painfully aware of all the things that had not happened in her life? Of all the things that would never happen? Of course, she might wear a wedding dress one day, but given the fact she was already the mother of a child, a tasteful suit would be more appropriate than the virginal white innocence of the gown in the picture.

She shot a surreptitious look at her visitor, and decided the question of her making the dress was probably, thankfully, largely theoretical.

Mrs. Pondergrove's gray wool coat was tidy and had probably been quite elegant in its day, but now it looked just a little worn at the cuffs and around the collar. The hat, too, was jaunty and elegant, but obviously old.

"A dress like this would take nearly a month of full-time work to make," Abby said, gently. "The fabric alone would cost a small fortune. And to do it justice, you would have to use very expensive beading on this bodice. The beading would all have to be done by hand."

"But you could do it?" the woman asked eagerly, as if she had not heard a single word Abby had said.

"I could sew this dress," Abby said slowly, "but I really think it would make more sense for you to go and buy one ready-made. I think it would be far less expensive."

"My dear, how touching that you would be concerned about an old lady spending her money."

"The truth is that the cost of making this dress would be extravagant."

"Oh, pooh. What is money for, except to make people happy?"

Reluctantly, Abby decided to burst the bubble. She named what she thought the dress would cost to make, including materials and a rough guess on her labor. She expected her visitor to flinch visibly, and was astounded when Mrs. Pondergrove beamed at her.

"When could you start, then?"

"You want to go ahead? At that price?"

"I most certainly do! When could you start on it?"

"Well, I guess I could start right away," Abby stammered.

"Good. Let me write you a check."

"Oh," Abby said. "Are you certain? You've never even seen my work."

"At my age, you can tell what kind of work people

do from the look in their eyes. You can tell all kinds of things from that. Take that young man who answered the door. I could tell he was as lonely as a camel on a cattle farm.''

''Really?'' Abby said, a little weakly.

''Oh, yes. He's heartbroken, that boy.''

Abby was not certain she had ever seen a person less likely to be called a *boy* than Shane McCall. And he seemed like about the least vulnerable man she had ever seen.

Though suddenly she thought of him telling her, that first crazy night, that he was a widower, and of the bitterness that had flashed briefly in his eyes when she had commented he seemed too young to have dealt with such a tragedy.

Bitterness? Or was that how a man like him would mask a broken heart?

''He thinks you mend a broken heart by putting a block of ice around it, but of course, nothing could be further from the truth.''

''That seems rather a lot to know about a person from one meeting,'' Abby said, and saw the shrewd eyes turned on her.

''You're right, of course,'' her visitor demurred. ''Now, how will we proceed on the dress? A check for the full amount?''

''Oh, no!'' Abby said. ''A down payment would be fine. A third now, and another third part way through, and a third at the end if you are completely satisfied. Who is the dress for? I'll need to contact her to arrange for fittings.''

''Fittings? No, I'm afraid that's not possible.''

''But—''

''The dress is a surprise, you see.''

"I can't make a dress without knowing who it's for! It won't fit correctly."

"Yes it will. Because the girl it is for is your size, *exactly.*"

"That's a strange coincidence."

"Isn't it?" Mrs. Pondergrove asked happily.

Abby looked at her visitor. She was lovely, but obviously eccentric. Was it possible she wasn't even all there? Could Abby, in good conscience, take her money? Maybe there wasn't even a bride!

"It must be for someone you love very much," Abby said, probing, hoping to get a little more information.

Instead, she found a check pressed into her hand, and she found herself looking into eyes that were young and strong and imminently sane.

"It's for someone to whom I owe a great debt," Mrs. Pondergrove said. "A debt that cannot be measured. I owe her happiness."

"No one could owe anyone else happiness," Abby protested.

"You are very young to realize something so wise." Mrs. Pondergrove sighed. "Still, one does what one can. I don't think white is quite right for that dress. You know what white represents these days is hopelessly old-fashioned. What do you think of ivory?"

Abby thought it made it a dress she could wear, after all. But she did not want to get attached to the dress, she did not want to think of herself in it for one moment. She suddenly wanted to refuse, but as a single mom she knew she could not base a financial decision that would affect her and Belle's well-being on emotion. Especially romantic, silly, wistful emotion.

"When do you need the dress by?" She heard a certain woodenness in her tone.

"Oh, they haven't set a date yet, but as soon as possible. Would you mind if I dropped by now and then to see how its progressing?"

"I'd be delighted."

Mrs. Pondergrove nodded with satisfaction. "I thought so. I can tell a great deal about you from your eyes, too."

"And what would that be?"

"Oh, I've jabbered quite enough for one day. I don't want you to dread me coming, to think, 'oh here comes that talkative old bag again,' when you see me coming up the walk."

"I would never think that," Abby said, and laughed.

After her guest had left, Abby took Belle across the hall to the kitchen. She realized she still had Mrs. Pondergrove's drawing in her hand, and she set it on the kitchen table. His notice about hours for kitchen use was posted on the fridge.

Neatly typed, it looked like a military itinerary. Underneath the itinerary were a list of rules about use of the fridge, also typed. The first requested her to label her food as belonging to her.

"Hungry," Belle announced impatiently.

She tore her eyes away from the list. "Honey, it looks like we're here illegally."

"Hungry," Belle repeated.

He had posted this time as his time to prepare lunch. Well, it would just have to go into effect tomorrow.

And sure enough she heard him coming down the stairs, but there was something off about the sound of the thumps. She heard him open the kiddie gate, instead of stepping over it.

He limped into the kitchen, and looked annoyed to see her there.

But she barely registered that. His knee was swollen up like a basketball.

"Did you read the schedule?" he asked, through gritted teeth.

"Just now. Is that what happened when you went over the gate?"

"Yes."

"Oh, Shane, I'm so sorry."

"It was my own fault. Could we go over this schedule? Does it look acceptable?"

"Well," she said, "it seems I have free rein of the kitchen, except for about an hour each day. I'm not going to complain, but what if you want a snack? Or a cup of coffee?"

The man's face was white with pain.

"I have an electric kettle upstairs. I don't snack."

"Oh. A man of complete self-control."

"That's correct."

"What are you going to do about your knee?"

"Put some ice on it, and take a pill."

"I think you need to see a doctor."

"Really?" His voice was like ice.

"Really."

"We will get along much better, until I have found new accommodations, if you don't give me advice."

"My apologies," she said with false meekness. "I'll just write that on the notice on the fridge, right under the rules about labeling."

"That would be good of you." His face suddenly went a whiter shade of white, and he limped over to a chair and sat down.

"I'll get you some lunch," she said. "What do you like? I bought peanut butter yesterday. Belle's favorite."

Peanut butter! She was offering this man peanut butter, as if he was two. She had been around her two-year-old a little too much. "I also make a mean omelette."

"I don't want you to get me lunch. I want you to get out of the kitchen, as per the posted schedule."

"It's the least I could do. It's my fault you hurt your knee."

"Thank you. I know."

"I just read the schedule. I didn't know it was your time."

"But you do now," he pointed out.

"Fine. Belle, we're leaving."

Belle was busy taking the bowls out of the cupboards. She looked up at her mother in horror and howled, "Belle hungry!"

"It's Mr. McCall's turn in the kitchen. You and I can walk downtown and get something."

"He feed me," Belle decided. "Sugar Pups." That decided, she went back to her bowls, happily nesting one inside the other.

"Oh, for God's sake, feed the kid," he said with great irritation, and then he sighed. "And while you're at it, I guess you could get me something, too. I have a package of bologna in the fridge."

Was he watching her with a certain humor in his narrowed eyes?

She squared her shoulders. She wasn't about to lie to him. "Not anymore, you don't."

"Really?" he said silkily.

"It was green in places!"

"Kindly don't throw out my belongings."

"You should thank me. I may have prevented you from death by food poisoning!"

"Maybe death by food poisoning was my preference over death by baby gate. I am a free man. I can eat deteriorating bologna if I want to."

She looked at him, and suddenly thought of Mrs. Pondergrove's remarks. Lonely as a camel on a cattle farm. Heartbroken.

"Humph."

"Pardon?" he said.

"Nothing."

So she made an omelette for him, which he thanked her for by scowling. She put Belle in her high chair, gave her some omelette too, and then sat down herself.

She saw the picture of the wedding dress was right in front of him, and that he was glaring down at it suspiciously.

"What is this?" he finally asked.

"My new job," she said.

He actually looked terrified. "Your new job is finding a husband?"

She wasn't quite sure how he had made that leap in logic. "No, the lady who came, Mrs. Pondergrove, asked me to make that for her."

"She's a little old for this dress," he said, his suspicion not dying.

Abby snatched the picture away from him, and said snippily. "Really? I didn't know people ever got too old to dream."

But suddenly she wasn't sure who she was talking about. Mrs. Pondergrove or herself.

Or maybe even him.

Chapter Five

"It's a foolish dress for an old woman," Shane said stubbornly. For some reason, when he had looked at the drawing, he had been able to picture Abby in that dress as clearly as if it were a photograph.

It reminded him of another dress, a long time ago, and a young woman coming toward him, the love shining in her eyes stilling the hammering of his heart.

"It's not for her to wear, obviously," Abby said, with a trace of annoyance.

Mrs. Pondergrove looked like the type who could be eccentric, able to overlook what was *obvious* even to him, about a dress like that. A dress like that was about believing in happily ever after.

"The omelette's pretty good," he said, but grudgingly. The truth was that after a steady diet of bologna and sardines, the omelette tasted like a little piece of heaven. And little pieces of heaven were just the things he needed to steel himself against.

Because he knew it was those little things that hurt

the most after. Stacey had made banana bread that he thought of now, craved, yearned for. Bologna did not make his mind wander to such memories.

"The secret is to use water," she said, reaching over and popping a little chunk of omelette in Belle's mouth.

"I thought you used eggs."

She rolled her eyes at him. Oh-oh. Something else that was obvious.

"Water instead of the milk," she said.

He decided he would not admit he had not known milk was an ingredient in an omelette. He'd thought omelettes were made with eggs and cheese. Period. But the omelette did not interest him nearly as much as the dress, and who it was for.

"So, she's not going to wear the dress. I assume she's not getting it made to hang it on her wall and look at it. Who is it for, then?" Really, he should leave it alone. But he could not get over the uneasy feeling that that dress was about Abby, somehow.

"Are you interrogating me?"

"No," he said sharply.

"Good."

"Who's the damned dress for?"

He saw the hesitation in her, saw her eyes narrow, knew she was going to tell him to mind his own business, which was what he deserved. It should, in fact, be posted on the rules. Mind your own business. But that's not what she said.

"Her daughter!" she finally replied triumphantly.

He'd been a cop long enough to be able to tell, most of the time, when someone was lying. Especially, someone like her, who was obviously not accustomed to lying. Her eyes were suddenly everywhere but on him.

Getting more omelette into baby Belle suddenly seemed to have become her life's mission.

"Gee," he said, "her daughter would only have to be about eighty."

"Mrs. Pondergrove is not *that* old!"

"Okay, maybe not that old, but her kids would have to be in their fifties. At least." That dress was about hopes and dreams and fairy tales. Even he, an idiot about such matters, could see that.

"Well, maybe its for her granddaughter then."

She was still very busy with that baby, wiping imaginary spots off Belle's face, while Belle flailed, trying to get away from her.

The dress, he thought, was for Abby. His gut had told him that the minute he had looked at it. That, and that book he'd spotted, meant she was on the hunt.

And with a belly button like hers, she should have absolutely no problem. Her top was lifting up and giving him a little peek at it every time she reached over to Belle.

Mrs. Pondergrove had probably come to see her about having a bit of lace put on her hat. Or a slip hemmed, or a button put on her jacket.

Without eating the rest of his omelette, which took considerable discipline on his part, he thanked her coolly for lunch, got up and limped out of the room.

By the next morning he knew she had taken the hint. The cupboards had been reorganized into His and Hers, labeled neatly with masking tape. The fridge shelves been bisected neatly down the middle with white wire dividers.

His side held a brand-new package of bologna and an unopened can of sardines. It made him look pathetic.

It also made him feel guilty that she had spent her

money on the bologna and the sardines when she had a child to support.

Well, he wasn't going to have to feel guilty anymore because he wasn't going to see her anymore. Or hear her, either. He had a brand-new CD Walkman player with earphones. He had bought some rank rock and roll music that he remembered fondly from his younger years. The majority of his fondness came from the fact that neither the music nor the lyrics could be considered conducive to romance.

He ate his breakfast, two pieces of burned toast, while listening to Acid Sam. He was annoyed, and somewhat startled to find he had matured. Acid Sam's vocals hurt his ears. And the lyrics hurt his spirit, which really didn't need further damage.

The kitchen seemed different. He wasn't quite sure how. Sure it was neat and tidy, but all she added was the magnets on the fridge.

No wait. The table had never had a cloth on it before. Bright red checks. Very homey and cozy. Not like an Italian restaurant at all.

He took a guilty swipe at his crumbs.

There it was again, despite all his efforts. Guilt. The feeling he despised as much as any other. The feeling that he had run all the way to Miracle Harbor to get away from. And it had caught up with him anyway. Her fault. Abby's. He took the Acid Sam CD from the player, broke it neatly in half and filed it in the garbage.

The blessed silence that followed was short-lived. He could hear the steady hum of what he assumed was her sewing machine, and she was keeping up a steady patter with Belle at the same time.

He wondered if it was hard to work with the baby around.

And since he was wondering about her anyway, he allowed himself to wonder, ever so briefly, if the top Abby was wearing today would show her belly button.

He heard his phone ring upstairs, climbed over the baby gate, and went to answer it. A prospective tenant he hoped.

And he was absolutely right. A construction worker named Harvey who thought he could talk his way around the "female only" part of the ad Shane had placed yesterday.

On the seventeenth call—all of them from construction workers—he unplugged his phone, and stared grimly out the window.

Little-her tumbled into the front yard in a bright red jacket that made her look as round as a beach ball. Right behind Belle came big-her pulling a red wagon with a few colorful boxes of bulbs in it. Soon the two of them were side by side, digging in the dirt, laughing.

After awhile big-her took off the plaid hooded jacket she was wearing.

His mouth went dry.

In a shirt that fit like that, who needed to see a belly button?

He thought the house needed a new rule: Thou shalt not show your belly button or wear tight fitting clothing of any kind. But then that might apply to him, too, and he was used to running around without his shirt on.

He had the oddest thought. What if his belly button affected her the same way that hers affected him?

Then, he decided, they would be in big trouble. Bigger trouble than he would know how to handle.

With a groan of pure misery, which he knew had nothing at all to do with his still swollen knee, he pulled down his shade and turned his phone back on.

* * *

Out of the corner of her eye, Abby saw the shade go down and felt mildly annoyed. She couldn't even put a few bulbs in the ground without irritating him? This was the third day in a row that she had come out into the yard to give Belle a little fresh air, and no sooner had they settled in at whatever project they were working on when his shade would go down.

"Oh, Abby," she chided herself out loud, "what makes you think it has anything to do with you? The sun is probably on his computer screen."

She lifted her face to the sun, and drank in the warmth of it. Spring came so much earlier here on the Oregon coast than it did in Chicago. But then she had learned the weather was always fairly mild here, winter temperatures only dipping down to about forty-five degrees.

"Not like Chicago," she said. When she had left, still it had been very much winter, bitterly cold and nasty.

Yet here, it was only March and the air was warm, tangy with earth smells, mixed with the scent of saltwater. After five days in Miracle Harbor, she was in love.

And not with the man upstairs, though her heart did odd things when she saw him in running shorts, which seemed to be the limit of his wardrobe. Well, so what? He'd had the very same effect on Mrs. Pondergrove. Probably had that effect on every female between the ages of eight and eighty.

One thing she definitely did not need in her life, ever again, was a man who all women found attractive.

Ty had been like a boy in a candy store when it came to women liking him. He grabbed whatever he could.

He'd even felt guilty about giving in to temptation, but had been unable to resist all the same.

"Honey, I just don't have any backbone," he told her with that lazy grin after she had found him in a clinch with a woman she had thought was her friend. She'd been six months pregnant at the time.

Well, if she was looking for one difference between the man upstairs and Belle's father, that would certainly be it.

There was no mistaking that Shane McCall had backbone, and plenty of it.

Even so, it was not him she was in love with. She had too much good sense for that.

No, she'd fallen in love with the town and the beauty of the Oregon coast. Her yard had a flowering quince in it, and also a camellia, both of them heavy with blossoms ready to burst. The pussy willow trees were getting fuzzy. The whole town was so quaint and pretty, and the people were friendly and helpful. It was really a town full of people just like Angel Pondergrove.

Twice she had taken Belle to the big town-center beach, which was only two blocks from their house. The ocean was incredible. Huge and mysterious, ever changing, sometimes whispering, sometimes crashing. Belle loved the sand, and though the weather was not yet conducive to swimming, Belle always managed to get good and wet before she was crammed, protesting, back in her stroller to go home.

Abby had worried about the availability of a good fabric store, but she needn't have. There were two, and both of them carried a nice selection. She had purchased a few yards of cheerful red-checkered cotton to brighten up the kitchen, and had whipped up a tablecloth, then hung some cafe-style curtains yesterday.

She had also purchased a bolt of ivory silk, delicate and shimmering as butterfly wings.

She had begun making the pattern for Mrs. Pondergrove's dress. She loved to sew, had been drawn to it since she was a small girl, when she had begun to make her own patterns for dolls, cutting the dresses out of leftover fabric of Judy's. She had been sewing her own clothes since she was a teenager, and had made a decent living making prom dresses and theatrical and dance costumes.

But nothing had ever felt like this dress. When she worked on it, she became so engrossed in it. Time and reality seemed to slip away.

Even now as she dug in the dirt with Belle, her thoughts went to the dress, constructing it step by step in her mind.

Just after one o'clock, she managed to pry Belle out of the dirt. They went into the kitchen for lunch, and she noticed, if he had been in here, there was no sign of it. Not a crumb on the table, or a smear on the counter.

She opened the fridge. The bologna package was nearly empty, evidence that she did share the house with someone else.

And then she noticed the scent in the room, subtle but powerful, and closed her eyes.

It was the scent of a man, wild and heady. Intoxicating.

She thought it would be in her best interests to add a little rule to his list.

Thou shalt not smell so good.

She laughed at her own silliness, made a quick lunch, and then put Belle down for her nap and took out the work she planned to do for the day. Within minutes

Belle was snoring and the sewing machine was humming.

Without even knowing that she did it, she began to sing. In her mind, she could see the slender back of the bride as she went down the aisle. Beyond her, at the altar, was the groom. It was *him*, Shane McCall, his eyes softened with the most incredible light. A tender smile playing across his face instead of that perpetual frown.

And then, without warning, the sewing-machine needle faltered, and then froze. The light mounted on the sewing machine flickered and went out.

Abby snatched her hand away from where she had been feeding the fabric and glared at the silk as if it was responsible for her ridiculous flight of fancy.

And then she heard him upstairs, cursing a blue streak. She reached out and flipped the light switch for the fixture above her head. Nothing. Despite the cursing upstairs, she was relieved the power had gone out, and nothing was wrong with her machine.

A moment later she met Shane McCall in the hall. He had a flashlight in his hand, and a familiar frown on his face. As if it was her fault the power had gone out!

Still, he had avoided her so scrupulously for days that she had almost forgotten the impact of him, live and in person.

Of course, he was wearing shorts, grey sweatshirt fabric, and a matching hooded sweatshirt. No emblem. She was too aware of his long bare legs, the muscle standing out in ridges on his thighs and in his calves. The bruise was almost gone from his shin, the swelling was down on his knee.

But his eyes had that same cool, impenetrable light in them.

"Everything okay upstairs? You sounded, er, upset."

"I yell, you sing."

"You can hear me singing?" she asked, mortified.

"Not often. Usually I have my own music on."

"Really? I've never heard it. I guess that's why I assumed you couldn't hear me."

"I use earphones."

"Oh." Was that a hint? "What do you listen to?"

"I'm trying classical."

"Trying it?"

"In recognition of my advancing age."

She had never seen a man who looked more in his prime.

"Well," she said, "you might want to try some Pachebel. He's my favorite. Good for bad tempers."

"I don't have a bad temper."

She raised an eyebrow at him.

"I just lost my whole morning's work."

"Don't you save?" He'd been listening to her singing. If there was a rock handy she probably would have crawled under it.

"Oh, sure. When I think of it. Which is usually when I'm ready to quit. You'd think I'd get it by now. This house's electrical system is crankier than an old Model T."

She wasn't happy to hear about that. If something major needed to be done, then what?

"I think its probably just a fuse," he said. "Why don't I show you where the fuse box is in the basement."

She had opened the door to the basement once, and decided against going down there. It looked dank and musty. She only had one debilitating fear in life but it was a gigantic one. She was phobic about spiders, and that basement looked, from her quick peek down the steps, like spider heaven.

"I think I'll take a pass on that," she said.

He folded his arms across his chest, and braced those legs wide apart. It made him look every inch a cop, even in the shorts. "No, you won't."

"Pardon?"

"Look, Abby, I'm not going to be here much longer. In fact, I'm interviewing some prospective tenants for my place tomorrow. So you need to know where the fuse box is." He sighed. "And also where the furnace is. And the storm windows."

"Oh," she said, her voice tiny. Somehow she had convinced herself that he would stay. She had glanced through the morning paper every day, and had seen there was not much available for rent. "You've found a new place then?"

"I've got a few places lined up to look at," he said vaguely.

"You don't have to find me a tenant. I can find my own."

He snorted at that.

"Well, I can!"

"Abby, this town if full of construction workers. I don't think you want to expose Belle to too much of that. Swearing—"

"Like she hasn't been hearing quite a bit of that lately."

A fascinating shade of pink moved up the column of his throat. "I'm used to living alone. I say rotten words when I feel rotten."

"That must be often!"

"As a matter of fact, it is."

"Why is that?"

"I have a shin the color of a plum, a toe with a nail about to fall off and a knee that feels like I went a round with someone with a baseball bat. I'm used to blowing off steam by running, and I haven't been out for nearly a week."

She knew he was evading her real question. He suddenly seemed fascinated with the switch on the flashlight.

"Why do you need to blow off steam?" she asked quietly.

"Because if I don't blow it off I feel rotten," he said smoothly, coming full circle.

"I meant, where is all that steam coming from?"

"I knew what you meant."

His eyes were on her face, intent, as if he actually was thinking of telling her something, and then he shrugged it off, rolling his shoulders like a prize fighter between rounds, and said, "Anyway, I feel responsible for you finding a good tenant. I don't want some guy moving in here who will throw wild parties and look lewdly at your belly button."

"My what?"

"Don't you have any shirts that tuck in?"

"Don't you have any pants with legs?"

For a moment, a hot animal awareness shimmered in the air between them. But then something flickered in his eyes and he said, "Let's have a look at that basement."

She hesitated but he had already moved on, and he shot an expectant look over his shoulder. "Come on."

She didn't want to tell him how afraid she was of spiders. The door to the basement was underneath the stairs. "You first," he said.

"Not on your life," she said. He was big enough to

take down at least most of the spiderwebs. She tucked in close to his back, and didn't move her eyes from a spot right between his shoulder blades.

The basement was horrible, she could tell by the smell. She still refused to look at anything but the reassuring broadness of his back. She followed him like a shadow across the basement, registering gloom, spooky shadows and dark places.

"So this is the fuse box," he said, shining his flashlight on it.

"This is not your first trip down here, is it?"

He laughed mirthlessly. "You'd better be prepared to make this particular trip a few times a month."

"Oh." She contained a shudder and looked around cautiously. It wasn't so bad. Plain concrete walls. A few empty wooden shelves. Nothing about this she couldn't handle.

"Have you seen a fuse box like this before?"

"Um-hmm," she said, scanning the walls more bravely now. Maybe she'd been given an old house without spiders in the basement. It was called Miracle Harbor after all.

"You can't see the fuse box from behind me."

She forced herself to step out from behind him. She looked obediently up at the fuse box.

"For this house, it's relatively new. Maybe twenty-five years old."

"That's good," she muttered. Caught in the flashlight beam, right above the fuse box, hanging from the roof, was a web glittering like it was spun of gold. She tried to look just at the fuse box, but her peripheral vision sharpened and noted that the cross-bridging on the ceiling looked like it had been decorated for Halloween. It dripped with webs.

''Now, if you look, you'll see the whole house is labeled. Upstairs bedroom, bath on this one. See this switch that's flipped?''

The spiderweb moved. Running down an invisible cord was the most immense spider she had ever seen— gray, small head, huge bulb-shaped body, hairy legs.

She flung herself against Shane, the scream primal.

''What the hell?''

But even as he said it, his arms tightened around her, and she could feel the strength in them, hear the hard reassuring beat of his heart where her head was burrowed into his chest.

She began to shake. ''I—I—I'm s-s-sorry. I—I—I'm s-s-scared of—''

To her humiliation, she began to cry when she tried to spit out the embarrassing truth.

''Shhh,'' he said, his tone surprisingly gentle, lifting her chin, searching her eyes. She had never seen his eyes look like that, and yet the expression seemed familiar.

Something beyond concern. Tenderness.

Just as she had imagined he might look if she came down the aisle toward him in a gown of pure ivory silk.

Something about the thought calmed her, and she drew in a deep hiccuping breath. She became aware that he smelled wonderful. That same aroma that she caught the occasional whiff of in the kitchen, now enveloped her. A tangy scent, wild, like a pine forest after a thunderstorm.

And she felt wonderful, too. Safe. More than safe. Feminine. Small against his largeness, soft against his hardness, her curvy lines fitting so nicely to his straight ones.

''It's okay,'' he said, drawing his eyes away from her

face, glancing around. "I won't let anything hurt you. Let's just get you upstairs. Thatta girl, take a deep breath."

She did, suddenly realized she was glued to him so tightly a piece of paper couldn't have passed between them, and reluctantly stepped back.

The spider dropped. She felt him land right on her shoulder. The world swung wildly around her, her vision turned red and then cleared and then turned red again. Then she felt the strength leech from her arms and legs.

Don't faint, she ordered herself. Pleaded with herself. And then the world went dark.

She slumped against him like a sack of flour, her body suddenly a deadweight. His arms automatically tightened around her.

His first reaction was that it had to be some kind of trick—something out of her book on man hunting.

But her head lolled back, her lips went slack and her face turned the whitest shade of white he had ever seen as her eyes rolled back in her head.

He scooped her up in his arms, noting she weighed practically nothing, and sore knee forgotten he went quickly up the stairs, and laid her limp body on the couch. He did a hasty first responder's check—taking her pulse, which was normal.

The girl had fainted, pure and simple.

He went through her apartment to her bathroom, registering, only obliquely, the tidiness of everything, the baskets of toys, the flower arrangements, the tasteful framed prints on the walls. She had created an atmosphere of cheerfulness. He dampened a facecloth in her sink, doing his best to ignore the row of lacy cupped bras that hung on her shower rod.

When he came back, he sat beside her on the couch, and put the damp cloth on her forehead. Her eyes fluttered, and then opened. She looked at him dazed, and then closed her eyes and groaned.

"Please tell me I didn't faint. Please."

"Well, if you didn't faint you had a massive cardiac arrest, so fainting probably isn't so bad."

"I'm not the fainting kind," she said fiercely. "Really."

"You've convinced me."

"It's just that I have this phobia. Spiders. I don't know why. I hate it. It's so weak and silly."

But what he was thinking was who the hell was going to go into the basement and look after fuses and such for her? The prospective tenants he had lined up to talk to tomorrow, after buying an answering machine so he could screen the applicants, were all women.

Still, he reminded himself, it was a brand-new age. One of them wouldn't be afraid of spiders. And would know all about fuses. And wouldn't be scared to hit the furnace, equally as cranky as the electrical system, in just the right place, with a wrench he kept down there just for that purpose. The successful applicant for his apartment would have to be able to go up the ladder to take the storm windows off and put the screens up, too.

This was a house that needed a man. Unfortunately.

"I feel like an idiot," she said.

When she struggled to sit up, he pushed her gently back down.

"You don't have to prove anything. Lay down for a minute." And she was a woman who needed a man, too. She even had a secret book that attested to that.

"I'm not trying to prove anything." She lay back down. Mutinously.

But she would probably never admit to it.

When he left her, a few minutes later, he felt as troubled as he had felt in a long time. She had, to this point, shown herself to be independent and very competent. She worked hard. That sewing machine hummed away all day, and part of the evening, too. In the face of her daughter's many demands, Abby seemed to remain unbelievably good-humored.

But the thing with the spiders made him very aware of an underlying fragility.

It wasn't that she needed someone to look after her. She would have been insulted at the very suggestion, and he recognized it did not quite fit.

It was something else.

She needed someone, not to take the load, but to share the load.

And he had the sinking feeling he could interview five thousand tenants and never find one like that.

Because she didn't need a tenant.

She needed a mate. A perfect mate.

Thank God he had no illusions about that being him. He had already failed completely and irrevocably in the perfect mate department.

Chapter Six

"So, when is the apartment going to be available? Can I have a look at it?"

Abby didn't dare look at Shane. And she didn't want to be too obvious in her study of her prospective tenant, either, sitting across from both of them at the kitchen table. She and Shane had been interviewing prospective tenants for a week now, during Belle's naptime.

Lola was almost completely bald, except for a purple strip of hair down the center of her head. She had three rings through her bottom lip, and more than Abby could count through her ears. The one through the eyebrow looked particularly painful.

"Did I mention I have a pet?" Lola asked, when no one answered her.

"No, I think you left that part out when I talked to you on the phone," Shane said, his voice cool, a certain dangerous note in it that Lola seemed to miss completely.

"Oh, well, it's not a dog or a cat or anything that

smells and leaves hair all over the place. It's an iguana. Iggy.''

Abby choked back her laughter. Shane glared at her.

''We don't allow dogs and cats,'' he said firmly. ''Or reptiles.''

''That sucks.''

''Yeah, well, life does sometimes.''

Lola picked up her bag, stood up, glared regally at both of them, and said, ''I think you're discriminating against me because of my age. You're just using Iggy as an excuse. I bet legally he doesn't even qualify as a pet. I might sue.''

''Actually,'' Shane said standing up and forming the policeman stance, ''it's only because of the iguana. You do share an entryway and a kitchen. Abby has a baby. She's fussy about what crawls around on the floor with it.''

''A baby?'' Lola said with abject horror. ''I can't stand babies. Thanks for wasting my time.'' And she marched out of the kitchen.

Abby was able to contain herself until she heard the front door slam, and then the first giggle slipped out.

''Don't,'' he warned her.

She bit her lip. But her shoulders shook. Then she gave up. She put her head down on the table and laughed. She laughed until it hurt, and then suddenly realized he was laughing, too.

''Oh, Shane, when she said the part about smoking marijuana for medicinal purposes I thought you were going to place her under arrest.''

''I don't have any jurisdiction in Oregon,'' he said glumly. ''Besides, I still was harboring this hope that maybe you could live with that if she knew what a fuse was.''

"And she thought—"

"It was a kind of bong."

"I'm not even sure I know what that is, exactly," Abby said. "Do you?"

"Ten years in law enforcement. Yeah, I know what a bong is. Drug paraphernalia." His stern look melted and he seemed to realize how hilarious their encounters had been. Shane began to laugh.

His laughter was pure, wonderful, like light coming into a dark place.

"And she," he managed to sputter, "was definitely the best of the candidates we've interviewed this week. How many?"

"Sixteen," she said. "And she was not the best one. I could have lived with that lady who coughed so much."

"It might have been catchy! Think about your child!"

"The woman with the cane seemed very nice."

"How the hell was she going to put up storm windows on the second floor?"

"I can do that!"

"Over my dead body."

"I could hire somebody."

"But you wouldn't."

"Shane," she said, "I'm perfectly happy with things the way they are. Aren't you? Where are you going to live if you leave here? In a houseful of people like her? There are worse things than me and Belle."

"I don't dislike you and Belle," he said, slowly. "I never meant for you to have that impression."

"Right! You avoid me like the plague. Except when we're interviewing possible replacements for you." Which she knew by now was going to be impossible, especially since he only seemed to be interviewing little old ladies. With a few wild young ones who slipped by his net and got through the front door by pure chance.

But even if they were interviewing guys, she was beginning to realize she would never replace him.

And how oddly empty her life would seem without him upstairs. And his package of bologna in the fridge.

"Abby, me avoiding you is not about you. At all."

"What's it about then?"

He looked away from her, the laughter gone from the room as suddenly as a rainbow going from the sky. "Me. It's about me."

She waited, knowing that the first threads of a relationship had formed over these past few days while they interviewed possible tenants together. A fragile thing was unfolding in front of her, and she waited, holding her breath.

"Abby, when Stacey died, my wife—" his voice faltered. "I just don't want to be around people anymore. I don't want to feel anymore."

She stared at him, her own heart breaking inside her chest at the look on his face, the strong features, for once, vulnerable. More than vulnerable.

"How long has it been?"

"Just over two years. Don't tell me I should get over it. I don't want to."

"You've made lonely a way of life, Shane."

"I guess."

"What if I promise not to make you feel anything?"

"You can't make a promise like that."

"Why not?"

"Because I'm already feeling all kinds of things."

It took all her courage to ask, but she asked. "Like what?"

"Like this." He got up out of his chair and came over to her. As he bent toward her, she knew it was coming, and she was powerless to move away from it.

Wanted it with her whole heart and soul.

His lips touched hers.

And all her own dark places—wounded places caused by betrayal and by love gone wrong—suddenly seemed to be drenched with light.

She had only seriously kissed one man in her whole life before. But her soul recognized the difference this time. Ty had taken. His kisses had been hungry and about him, about filling some need in him.

But this, her lips meeting Shane's, was something else all together.

It felt like some place within her that had been held in chains was suddenly free, soaring high above all the trials and insecurities and pains of being human. This was the other side of being human, the side every woman dreamed of and hoped for in some secret place within herself. This was the glorious side, the place where all that was human in her took wing and touched the place of the gods.

She twined her arms around his neck, pulled him closer to her, allowed the kiss to deepen. She felt the power in his arms, and the passion in his soul, as he gathered her to him with a moan of surrender and despair.

He pulled away, suddenly, leaving her gasping and looking at him with naked desire that she could not hide.

"I'm sorry," he said, looking away from her and running a hand through his hair.

"Sorry?" she whispered. Sorry was somehow the last thing she was feeling.

"That's why we can't stay under the same roof."

"Oh. Of course."

He looked at her long and hard, troubled, and then he brightened. "Wait, I've got it."

"What?" she asked, though she did not want to know how he had solved what he saw as a dilemma and she saw as a gift from heaven.

"I know where to find you a perfect person to share this house."

"And where would that be?" She felt as if she was getting cold, as if every ounce of warmth had drained from the room, as if she had been swept up in the elating and electrifying power of a sudden summer storm, but was now left only drenched and shaking.

"A church," he said triumphantly. "I can't exactly see Lola hanging out there on a Sunday morning, can you?"

"No," she said woodenly.

Belle, waking up from her afternoon nap, began to cry.

"Pop her in the stroller. St. James's is right around the corner. We'll see if they have a bulletin board or something."

She told herself to say no. But she didn't. She said yes. And then felt pathetic. Was she willing to do anything just to be with him?

Yes.

This was not looking good. At all.

Shane could not believe what had just happened. He'd kissed Abby. In the kitchen. And her lips had been the sweetest thing he had ever tasted. Ever. He felt like he had been walking in a desert, parched, without hope, and she was an oasis, her lips a sweet fruit that quenched the thirst that had been all-consuming within him.

Which only meant he'd been right all along.

He had to get away from her. From the temptation of her, from the appeal of her. Posting a note at the church was a brainstorm.

Why had he asked her to come along?

He hadn't been thinking. It was completely unnecessary for her to make the trip, too.

Did he want to be with her?

Yes.

All the more reason that notice had to go up at the church and now. She needed someone. He knew that. She wanted to be independent, she was independent, but her life would be easier if she was sharing it.

Belle was a handful.

And so was this old house.

It's just that someone could not be him. She needed someone with a heart that was whole, not torn to pieces. She needed someone who would love only her, not someone who was in love with a ghost.

In love with a ghost. He thought about that for a moment and recognized it was not quite true. He had loved his wife while she lived. And resented her heartily since she died. Resented her for the jumble of emotion inside of him, for the huge cracks in the veneer of his strength. Resented her for showing him that he was not infallible.

But most of all he resented her because of what she had made him. A failure.

He had failed to be there when she needed him.

Failed to save her.

Abby did not need a man with that kind of baggage.

A man capable of failure, especially a failure of such a gargantuan proportion. A failure in such a crucial area.

He went up to his desk, pulled his notepad to him and wrote: Wanted: Tenant for upstairs apartment. Shared kitchen. He did not, with great discipline, add what he most wanted to add. Female only. If the last sixteen people they had talked to were any indication, a female who was good with fuses was as rare a find as a gorilla who could tap dance.

But if a nice church-going boy came along who could change a fuse and who did not have a history of not being where he should have been in a life-and-death moment, then that is what Abby deserved.

But it felt to Shane like he was tearing what was left of his own heart out when he tore that piece of paper from the pad.

She was just coming into the front hall when he came back down the stairs. She turned and smiled at him, her eyes cautious.

The caution, he knew, was brought on by his stupid kiss by the new tension crackling in the air between them.

Belle was not nearly so cautious. She stood up in her stroller, she was so excited to see him. Why did she care about him so much? Weren't babies supposed to have some kind of instinct that told them who people really were? Or maybe that was dogs.

"Up?" she crowed, holding out her arms to him.

"Belle, sit down before you fall down," Abby said. "No, up."

Belle ignored her mother, and he was helpless before her. He went and picked her up.

"I can carry her. We don't need the stroller."

Belle wrapped her arms around his neck and gave

him a big sloppy smooch on his cheek. Now he'd been kissed more today than he had in the past two years.

"Are you sure you want to carry her? She's heavier than she looks."

"Yeah, I'm sure."

Abby went out the door and down the walk first, and then he directed her which way to go.

He supposed they looked like a family walking down the street, the baby crowing and pointing at a cat slinking along through the shrubs beside them.

"Name," she demanded.

"Cat," he said.

Abby laughed, a little self-consciously. "It's a game we play. I name all the animals for her."

"Really? Like what?"

Abby shot the cat a look. "He looks like a...Mr. Snotgrodden."

"Not you," Belle said officiously. "He." She pulled at his shirt so he couldn't make a mistake.

"Oh." He looked at the cat. "How about Rags?"

Belle frowned at him.

"The more syllables the better," Abby whispered to him.

"Oh. How about Bottomsworth?"

Belle smiled, pleased that he had caught on so quickly, while he debated whether or not that was a Freudian slip of the perverted kind.

Who had a worthier bottom, after all, than the woman beside him?

"Walk now," Belle said. After a glance at her mother, he set her down. In short order he became aware the walk to the church was going to take somewhat longer than he had anticipated. Belle crouched down and inspected *everything*. Dried worm bodies, used Popsicle sticks, leaves. All were scrutinized, and explanations demanded.

Out of the blue it hit him, like a punch on his blind side.

If Stacey had lived, this might have been his life. Out for walks. Their baby would have been about this age now. Full of curiosity, and life and wonder.

There it was. That familiar feeling of being crushed under the weight of his own feelings. It wasn't just Abby who needed someone without baggage, it was that baby. She needed a man who could look at her without mourning his own losses.

Belle pointed to something, and proclaimed loudly, "Poop. Don't touch!"

Despite himself, he smiled. They learned all the important things really young. The church was just up ahead, the hall beside it. There was a bulletin board on the exterior hall wall, and he went and posted the notice.

"Do you want to go in for a minute?" Abby asked.

"To the church? Why?"

"I don't know. I like churches. They always smell so good and feel so peaceful inside. Ever since I was little I would ask God to look after my real Mom, wherever she was. And maybe she was up there with Him, looking after me."

Her words reminded him he was not the only one who had suffered losses.

So he shrugged, and followed her up the wide stone steps to the church entry. He hoped it would be locked. The policeman in him thought it should be locked. But, of course, it wasn't.

As soon as he stepped inside, he knew it had been a mistake. He was not a church kind of guy. In recent years he'd only been in one twice. The same one.

He'd married her.

And buried her.

He hesitated as Abby took Belle firmly in hand, and went up the aisle. She stopped at a pew, slid in, looked at the altar. The light from a stained-glass window was falling over her face, and it made her look incredibly beautiful.

She bowed her head and folded her hands together.

Feeling awkward, he slipped into a pew at the back of the church to wait for her. The hush and the smell blended together. He closed his eyes. She was right. It was a peaceful place.

Maybe too peaceful. He could feel his head drooping against his chest. Too many nights of the "bear went over the mountain" running through his head. He hated to think what the additional memory of her lips was going to do to his sleep patterns.

He felt her before he saw her. Stacey.

She looked beautiful, her long dark hair free, wearing a dress that was long and flowing and white. He felt so happy to see her.

But she didn't look at all happy to see him.

In fact she had her hands on her hips in a position he remembered very well. He'd been treated to it on several occasions. Like when, newly married, he'd gone for a few drinks after a hard shift and had forgotten to call.

"You're a real jerk," she said.

Somehow he had not pictured this as being the tone for their reunion. He wanted to speak to her, but couldn't, his tongue lead inside his mouth.

She glared at him. "Look, Shane, I can't stand you like this. Full of self-pity. Full of yourself."

He wanted to protest, but again he found his tongue

heavy within his mouth, without words, his lips glued shut.

"That young woman is all alone here in this town. She doesn't know a single soul. Her sisters aren't here yet. She's with that baby all day. That's harder than it looks, you know. It's not all kisses and cuddles. And you won't even be her friend. What's the matter with you?"

He'd somehow forgotten this side of Stacey. Once, he'd come home to find a bust he'd been on had been televised, and she had been furious with him. Said he had been *mean*, unnecessarily rough. When he'd tried to tell her the bad guy had tried to blow his head off, she'd sniffed and said, "So that's all the excuse you need to become the bad guy?"

He'd never forgotten that. It had changed him in some fundamental way, made him a better cop and a better man.

Stacey's look suddenly softened, and with the white dress floating around her, she came toward him. "This isn't the Shane McCall I loved. The Shane McCall I loved always tried to do the right thing."

She turned and walked away from him, tossing her hair over her shoulder. Then she turned back and came up to him, took his shoulders, and shook them. "Wake up," she said.

"Shane, wake up."

"Huh?" He started awake, and saw Abby looking at him, smiling wryly.

"I'm ready to leave," she whispered.

He clambered to his feet. "I must have dozed off," he said, feeling groggy and disoriented. "Sorry."

"You don't have to be sorry."

"I wasn't talking to you."

She gave him a baffled look and he shook his head to clear the last of the cobwebs away. He reached down and picked up Belle, and walked down the aisle of the church. Belle liked what the patterns of light the stained glass threw on the floor.

Out in the sunshine, Abby scanned his face. "I told you it was peaceful," she said with a smile. "I didn't know you'd find it quite that peaceful."

"Yeah." No point telling her it hadn't been all that peaceful for him. "Sometimes I nod off during the day. I don't always sleep very well at night."

"Since I came?" she asked, stricken.

"No."

"Since your wife died?"

"Yeah."

"You must have loved each other very much."

"Yeah."

"How did she die, Shane?"

"She fell down some steps. When I wasn't home." He should have been home that day, but a call had come from work and he'd gone. "She was eight months pregnant."

He wished he wouldn't have added that, because Abby's eyes filmed over with tears, and her hand touched his arm. She didn't say one single word, and he was so grateful to her for that.

He cleared his throat.

Do the right thing.

He thought he had been doing the right thing. Keeping his distance, staying out of her hair, keeping himself free of entanglements.

"Have you, er, met anyone yet? Here?"

"Oh." She looked embarrassed. "I don't get out much. You know, with Belle and everything."

"You haven't even met any other young moms, at the park, or something?"

She looked away from him swiftly, but not before he caught the glitter in her eyes. When she turned back to him she was smiling with false brightness.

"There's always Mrs. Pondergrove," she said, "And my sister, Brittany will be here by the end of the month. I talked to her on the phone the other night and guess what?"

"What?"

"She's scared to death of spiders!"

"You're kidding, right?"

"I can't tell you how I felt when I heard that."

He could see how she felt from the gentle glow in her eyes. Not so damned alone in the world.

"There are worse things than being afraid of spiders," he told her gruffly.

"Name one!"

Being afraid of life. "I knew a cop once who was afraid of needles. Big guy, too. Bigger than me. We got a call from the hospital one time, after a car accident. Little kid needed a ton of blood. The rare kind. I've got it, so did he. He fainted dead as soon as they stuck the needle in his arm."

"Really?" she said, obviously pleased.

"A phobia is not like a character defect," he told her. "That man was one of the most courageous people I ever served with."

"Thanks, Shane."

"I'm not a complete jerk."

She gave him a surprised look. "Who ever called you a jerk?"

"Somebody who knows a jerk when they see one." He sighed. "Do you want to go and get a bite to eat?"

He wasn't sure what it meant when her face lit up. He only knew he felt completely unworthy of it.

Walking beside him, Belle now on his shoulders yelling her delight at the new view from up there, Abby allowed herself to feel content.

This is what her life might have been. Had she stayed with Ty. The nice family outings. Mommy, Daddy, baby, that grouping of three that she had so come to envy.

Not that she had any illusions about Ty ever being able to fit into that particular picture.

"Monogamy is not in my nature," he had told her, when she'd caught him. "And if any man tells you it is in his nature, he's a liar."

She felt herself pull away from the man beside her at that memory, and then she relaxed. She wasn't having a relationship with Shane McCall. He'd made that very clear.

Could a man and a woman be just friends?

An idea Ty would have scorned.

But what was wrong with just being in the moment? Never mind spoiling it by analyzing what might or might not happen down the road. What about just enjoying the sweetness of this uncomplicated moment?

They walked to a little cafe by the ocean. It was still too early in the year to sit outside, with the blustery wind blowing off the harbor, so they went in. They ordered sandwiches for themselves and a hot dog for Belle, which was a mistake. She removed the hot dog from the bun, took a bite and then threw it on the floor in distaste. She proceeded to squish the bun between her fingers, and soon had relish, ketchup and mustard spread from her forehead to her neckline. Only when the bun had been mashed flat and bore an unfortunate resemblance to roadkill, did Belle take a bite.

"Yum-yum," she declared.

Shane hooted with laughter. It was only the second time Abby had seen him laugh, and she thought the sound of it, the way it stripped the years from his face and the haunted look from his eyes, might make his laughter something she could become addicted to.

After lunch, he bought a kite at a little souvenir shop next to the restaurant and they went to the beach, to fly it.

Running along the beach, laughing, watching that kite, Abby was not sure she had ever felt so carefree, so wonderful, so alive.

Later, walking home, tired, Belle nearly asleep in the crook of his arm, she felt his hand rest on her shoulder, just for a moment.

When they paused at the entryway he handed her the now sleeping child, and looked at her long and hard.

For an exhilarating moment, she thought he might kiss her again, but he didn't.

He smiled, shook his head introspectively, and went up the stairs.

Chapter Seven

There they were, little-her and big-her, out in the yard, earlier today than usual. Shane was watching out his window that overlooked the front yard. Today, Abby had a shovel. At first he found it a little amusing watching her.

She stamped the shovel into the grass with determination, and when that produced no result she jumped on it with both feet. The shovel went into the ground about an inch. She jumped on it again. And then again.

He wasn't sure what she was doing, but it was going to take her a while. Belle had her own little shovel and had plunked herself down near some dirt and was busy digging a hole. She was better at it than her mother.

Abby had already taken off her jacket and wiped her brow. Jeans today, and a man's shirt over a T-shirt, her Cubs hat on backwards. She looked like the teenage boy he had mistaken her for at first. Abby jumped on the shovel again. He hoped she wasn't going to hurt herself.

He shook his head, and turned back to his computer.

Staring at the screen, he read over the three sentences he had written this morning, and then looked out the window again. She had managed to loosen a hefty piece of sod, and was trying to tear it off with her hands. Either she shouldn't be bending over like that, or he shouldn't be looking.

He made himself look back at his screen. Hunting and pecking, he typed out the next line of the chapter. Only what appeared on his screen was *You're a real jerk.*

With a sigh, he backspaced over that, saved his hard won three lines and went down the stairs and outside.

"Do you need a hand?" he asked her.

"No," she said, panting, standing on top of her shovel.

"What are you doing?"

She stepped down from the shovel. "I want to extend this flower bed. But the grass is in the way."

"It would probably take me ten minutes to get it out of your way."

"It's all right, I can do it."

He saw now where she had marked a curved line on the grass with something white. It looked suspiciously like flour. She jumped on her shovel again.

"You're going to hurt yourself," he said.

"No, I—Belle, don't eat that!" She dropped the shovel and ran over to her daughter, who was about to ingest a worm.

He picked up the shovel. And started digging, noting his knee seemed to be completely healed. In ten minutes he had the sod stripped, and the ground turned.

"Equal rights aside," he said, handing her back the shovel, "men were made to do certain things."

"I can't believe you could do that so quickly," she

said a little glumly. "It makes me feel terribly inadequate."

"I bet there's lots of things you're better at than me," he said.

"Like what?"

"The kitchen smells pretty good after you've been in there."

"It does after you've been in there too," she said.

"What? You like the smell of sardines?"

She blushed fiery red, and turned away from him. "Tell you what. I'll thank you for the flower bed with lunch. How would that be?"

That would be impossible, he thought. They couldn't start sharing that kitchen. But that isn't what he answered her.

He said, "That would be just fine. Do you want anything else dug up while I'm here?" She made him sorry he had asked. She wanted half the yard excavated. A small vegetable garden here, a few herbs right there, a little curving walkway in between them.

"Of course," she said, suddenly embarrassed, "I don't expect you to do that. Really, I don't. In fact, I'd rather do it myself."

"How about if I just see what I can get done before lunch? After that I'll surrender the shovel to you."

She mulled that over for a moment. "That would be fair. Belle, you come with me. We'll go in and make some lunch."

"No, Belle stay with he!" Belle informed her, not looking up from her energetic digging in an existing flower bed.

"I don't mind keeping an eye on her."

Abby's mouth dropped, and then she looked at him

narrowly. "It's harder than you think. You can't let her put things in her mouth."

"Trust me. I've protected my nation from numerous bad guys. Very bad guys. I can probably manage a baby."

She smiled and relaxed. "Yes, you probably can. I'll call you when lunch is ready.

He nodded and set to work, watching Belle out of the corner of his eye. After a while he began to feel like a tape recorder because he'd yelled, "Don't eat that!" so often. In the persistence department he didn't think very many bad guys would be able to hold a candle to little Miss Mischief, who in between trying to eat dirt, rocks and worms also made three attempts to escape from the yard. She hooted with laughter each time she made him drop the shovel and come after her.

Finally, he planted her and her shovel right in front of him. "Don't move," he told her, and realized that order was like telling a river not to flow, or the wind not to blow. The kid was in constant motion. He finally realized that what she really wanted was his undivided attention.

He put down the shovel and sat down on the grass. After a moment, she toddled over and sat beside him.

She was eager to show him a worm she had just found, and also a leaf. The leaf looked half-rotten to him, but was endlessly fascinating to her. She garbled away about it for a few minutes, and though he didn't understand a word, he nodded his head and told her it was very nice. Apparently satisfied, she went back to the patch of earth he had designated for her and began to dig again.

And sing. "Bear odor da mowin, bear odor da mowin, see, see, see, seeeeee."

He worked for half an hour or so, enjoying the little girl's company, and all the strange treasures she brought over for his approval. A rock, a snail, some twigs, an old rusted ball bearing. He turned over each item in his hands, and found for some odd reason, his interest was not pretended. Belle had a way of making him see things in a brand-new way.

And to rediscover old things, too. He became aware of the smell of the freshly turned earth, remembered how much he had always liked that smell, and even this kind of work. The shoveling put a pleasant strain on his muscles, and between that and a mellow spring sun, the sweat trickled down his forehead. He felt content.

Abby opened the kitchen window. It groaned, and she could only get it open an inch or two. Something else that needed to be fixed.

"Lunch," Abby called.

He lifted Belle onto his shoulders. She insisted he gallop around the yard three times before she allowed him to take her into the house.

Abby took her from him at the door.

"Is there a girl under all that dirt?" she asked.

"No!" Belle crowed, delighted to be disguised, but not so delighted when her mother hauled her away to clean her up.

Shane went upstairs and washed up, and as an afterthought, reapplied his deodorant.

A concession to living in a house with a woman.

When he came back down to the kitchen they hadn't returned, though he could hear Belle squealing protests about being subjected to her mother's vigorous cleaning. He acknowledged he felt a little weary, and not from digging. There really was more to raising a child than kisses and cuddles. He wondered how Abby managed it every single day without a break.

The kitchen smelled of heaven—garlic and spices heavy in the air.

The newspaper was open on the table, and he went and glanced at it, then wondered if there was anything in particular Abby had been looking at on this page.

Then he saw it. An full color ad for a red-and-white swing and slide set, with a covered sandbox. Had she been looking at that? Wishing she had it for Belle?

Thinking about getting it but knowing she had no way of putting it together? She probably didn't even have the money for it. Was his rent her only income? Besides sewing flowers on old lady's hats? That couldn't bring in too much.

He closed the paper just as Abby and Belle came into the room. Belle was in a clean denim jumper, with little blue leotards over her plump legs. Abby had removed the Cubs hat and done something to her hair. Gelled it so that it stuck up in cute little spikes. If he was not mistaken her lips were shiny, too. Gloss?

For him? A concession to living with a man? Come to think of it, both of them smelled good too—of soap and soft feminine things that reminded him of spring.

Was he getting himself into trouble here?

The smell of garlic and good things cooking lured him forward even as his mind warned him to go back.

Lunch tasted better than it had smelled, which hardly even seemed possible.

"It's just casual," she said, blushing when he complimented her. "Caesar salad and Tetrazzini."

"Are you kidding? Casual is bologna and sardines."

She laughed. She looked wonderful in that too-large

shirt, tied at the waist and sleeves rolled up, a tight red T-shirt on underneath it. Red suited her. Why?

Did it hint at something red-hot just below that calm "somebody's mommy" surface?

Belle was demanding to know why these worms were okay to eat, but not the ones outside. Because of her limited use of language it took her most of lunch to make her point. He could have lingered forever, entertained by this impromptu game of mother and daughter charades.

Instead, he suddenly remembered the appointment he'd made for that afternoon. He glanced at his watch. The appointment that begins in five minutes.

He prided himself on never forgetting appointments.

Of course, until very recently, he had nothing to clutter up the order of his life.

A young guy had called him and said he'd seen the ad for the suite on the church bulletin board. Shane had decided not even to involve Abby in the interview.

He was looking for something quite different than she was.

He wanted to be assured that whoever took over his suite could help her out with windows that didn't open, and grass that didn't budge until more than ninety-seven pounds of force was applied to it. She would be indignant at the very idea that she needed help.

"Thanks for lunch," he said, "but I've got to run. I just remembered something I have to do this afternoon."

Did she look disappointed?

"Thank you for digging my bed for me"

He could be stripped of the Boy Scout badge he had just earned for the thought that went through his head about what he'd like to be doing in her bed. And it had nothing to do with digging. Or flowers either.

Still, despite that one renegade thought, he felt strangely good about what had just happened. He knew what he had experienced in the church had just been a dream, but in it had been the kernels of a truth he needed to know about himself. It was one thing to be a hermit, it was another to be a jerk.

Abby was a single mom, and she needed a bit of support. That kid was exhausting without Abby tackling the yard and a job, too. So, he could give her a hand every now and then. Until the new guy took over. The truth was he felt better. Handling that shovel for her had done him as much good as it had her.

Lunch was a bonus.

Because he was running a little late, he drove to the cafe. It was the same one where he and Abby and Belle had had lunch, and he felt like their laughter over Belle and that hot dog still lingered there.

He had just been served coffee when he was joined at the table.

"Mr. McCall, sir?"

"That's me."

"David Hathoway."

The young man looked to be in his early twenties. He was slight and blond, wearing plastic rimmed glasses that made him look like a *real* Boy Scout. He appeared to be clean-cut, wholesome, owlish.

Shane took the young man's proffered hand and shook it, didn't let it register in his face that the handshake was disappointing.

"Have a seat, David. Coffee?"

"Oh, no, I don't use anything with caffeine in it. I consider caffeine a drug."

Perfect. No marijuana for medicinal purposes. Still, Shane took a rebellious sip of his own caffeine-laden cappuccino. "So, David, you saw my ad on the church bulletin board?"

"That's correct. I'm staying with the minister right now, because of the housing shortage. I'm signed up for a bible course he's teaching."

Bible course. Perfect again. He wouldn't be stealing Belle's Sugar Pups from the cupboards, or helping himself to the Gouda.

"Are you handy?"

"Handy, sir?"

"A single woman lives in the ground floor suite. The yard needs some work and she wants to put in a garden. She's got a landscaping plan that she doesn't quite have the muscle to execute." Not that she'd ever admit it.

"I wouldn't mind helping with the yard at all. I'd love to help put in a garden. We always had one at home on the farm."

Shane wasn't quite sure how to tell David he might have to wrestle the shovel from her body. Maybe he'd see how this went, and get to that part later in the interview.

"It's an old house. The fuses blow, the windows don't like to open, the furnace needs a good hard kick every now and then. And you can't let her go in that basement at all."

Shane wasn't quite sure how to make it clear how imperative that was. Maybe he'd get back to that part later, too.

The kid smiled eagerly, "Oh, I'm great at stuff like that. Our farmhouse was over a hundred years old. My mom calls me a regular Mr. Fix-it."

"And what does your girlfriend call you?" Was that

subtle enough? He was interviewing a tenant for Abby, not a potential husband. Which didn't exactly explain why he was so relieved the boy was obviously too young for her. What did he care if David had a girl-friend?

But if David had a girlfriend it might help him keep his eyes off Abby's belly button. Shane was surprised at how much he didn't like the idea of anybody else looking at her belly button, too young for her or not.

Not that he seemed to be able to keep his own eyes where they belonged, not if his life depended on it.

"Well, sir, I'm not currently in a relationship. But if I was, my girl would never see the inside of my apartment. Not until we were married. I wouldn't throw myself on temptation's door like that."

"Oh. Okay." A decent, old-fashioned boy. The boy least likely to sneak a peek, steal the cereal or have wild parties. A boy who looked like he would be eager to help out around the place.

"The rent has to be paid right on time, no excuses."

David looked injured. "I've been saving my money for a year to do this. I plan to get a part-time job, too."

That settled it. Shane had found the perfect tenant.

Why did he feel sick inside? Was it because he really, deep down, didn't want to move? Had enjoyed that day of kite flying, not to mention the little encounter in the backyard more than he wanted to admit? Not to mention Tetrazzini and Caesar salad? And looking at worms in a brand-new light?

"Like I said, your landlady lives downstairs. You'd be sharing a kitchen with her and a front entry hall. You have to be careful with the front door and you have to leave a baby gate up, so that Belle doesn't go outside or up the stairs."

"Belle?"

"Her kid. The landlady's baby."

"Is she married? The landlady?"

Shane looked at him narrowly. David better not be getting any ideas about romancing the landlady. "Why do you ask?"

"I live by a certain moral code." An interesting thing was happening to the boy's face. It was getting all pinched looking around the mouth.

"As a matter of fact, Abby's not married," he said, danger in his voice.

"A widow, I hope."

"That's a funny thing to hope for someone."

"Divorced?" David said.

"No."

The kid missed the warning note completely. "Well, I can't live in a house with a woman of loose morals."

Shane felt like he was going to pick him up and throw him through the picture window at the front of the restaurant.

"Really?" he managed to say, his voice ice-edged.

Again, David seemed to miss the dangerous footing he had moved into, so eager was he to share his self-righteous judgements. "I don't approve of women who have children out of wedlock."

"Is that right?"

"It is."

Somehow, by some thread, Shane's temper held. "I'm not much into this stuff, but I could have sworn there was a part in that book you've come to study about throwing the first stone."

Shane got up and tossed a bill on the table for the coffee he had barely touched. He turned on his heel and walked out. He gave himself a pat on the back for managing not to have that kid's shirt wrapped around his fist, slamming him up against a wall.

Stacey would have called that mean, recognized it as lowering himself to the same level as that creep sitting in there disguised as Mr. Decent. Shane got in his vehicle, then noticed the hardware store was right down the street. Was that the same one that had advertised the swing set? It wouldn't hurt to go check it out.

He came back out with a bulky box on his shoulder. Really, when he thought about it, there was no rush to rent the upper part of the house. He might as well wait until he had found decent accommodations elsewhere.

Which, admittedly, might take a while.

"What are you doing?" Abby asked, coming up behind him as he worked on the yard. He had all the pieces of the swing set lying on the grass, and he'd hauled his tool kit out of the basement. He perused the instructions only briefly, before crumpling them up and rubbing his hands together. Any moron could see what step came first.

"Nothing," he said, confidently bolting the cross piece to the A-frame.

She looked at the box. "A swing set?"

"Cute, isn't it? Kind of like a barber's pole." He fastened the second cross piece, and frowned.

"I think that's backward," she said.

He studied it. Damned if she wasn't right. He didn't want to uncrumple the instructions in front of her, so he quickly undid it and put it the right way.

"Shane, the swing set is for?"

"I got it for Belle." He dared her to make something of that. "Can you grab that end, and we'll stand this part up?"

Her mouth fell open. "Shane. I wish you wouldn't have. It's too much."

"You wanted one for her, didn't you?"

She looked amazed. "I've never given it a thought."

He frowned and tightened a bolt. She must have been looking at something else on that page of the newspaper.

"Well, do you think Belle will like it?"

"She'll adore it," Abby admitted reluctantly.

"Great," he said. "Could you hand me that half inch wrench?"

For a man who seemed to be digging himself in deeper, he couldn't deny this funny feeling inside himself. It had been so long since he had felt it, that at first he didn't recognize what it was. Happiness. He started to whistle. The swing set took him five hours to assemble and then he had to push Belle, who squealed with glee, for a half an hour. But it made every second it had taken him to put that monster piece of equipment together worthwhile.

He slept better that night than he had slept in years. In the morning he noticed yesterday's paper still sitting on his desk and just out of curiosity, he opened it to the ad for the swings.

On that same page were bridge scores, a supermarket display ad featuring toilet paper, an article and picture about some old gent's hundredth birthday. On the opposite page was a story and picture about the deplorable eyesore the old cannery was. Shane noticed the paper seemed to run that article and picture, unchanged, once a month or so.

And then he saw a very small piece about Friday night being the last night the local theater company was presenting their comedy, *The Hen House*. Had she wanted to see the play?

What would it hurt to ask her? Poor girl never got out.

"A play? On Friday?" Abby said. She put a pin in the cushion she had attached to her wrist, trying to disguise the fact her heart had just tried to leap out of her chest. "Me?"

"Just you."

"I love the theater," she said, and then was sorry. She looked everywhere but at him. "No. I couldn't possibly."

"Why not?"

"I don't have a baby-sitter," she said, which was true, even though any excuse would have done.

"Ask that old gal in the hat. I bet she'd do it."

"Mrs. Pondergrove? I don't know, Shane." Abby thought those were probably the very hardest words she'd ever spoken.

"What's the problem? You said you love the theater. When's the last time you went and did something just for grown-ups?"

"It's been a while," she admitted, and hoped that didn't reveal too much about the pathetic loneliness of her life. Not that she didn't love Belle, not that she'd change a thing, but...

Actually, there was a real reason she didn't want to go. She was working on that dress. The silk, despite being so difficult to work with, especially with Belle wanting so desperately to "help," was coming alive under her fingertips, taking shape each day. Singing to her heart.

About dreams. And romantic notions.

About the man upstairs.

Her thoughts always drifted to him when she sat down with those yards of ivory silk. At first it had been innocent enough. She would hear him upstairs, and try to imagine what he was doing, and what he was wearing and what he looked like.

Was his brow furrowed in concentration? Did he stick his tongue out between his teeth all the time when he concentrated, the way he had when he worked on that swing set?

But then her thoughts would drift a little further, and her tummy would begin to tingle, especially if she thought of how he had looked with that shovel, his muscles rippling, the sweat forming a fine sheen on his skin, the way he'd thrown back his head and laughed when Belle had compared her Tetrazzini to worms.

As she worked on the dress, she remembered how being near him made her feel all quivery inside, as if she had been asked to speak in front of an audience of five hundred.

And then her thoughts would drift further yet, down that river of fantasy, getting further and further from reality. She would rethink that brief kiss, and relive it.

Sewing that dress, she would think forbidden thoughts of what it would be like to be his bride, to walk down an aisle and to see his eyes on her.

And then to go into his bed at night, to feel his lips on her lips, and on her cheeks and on, well, everything.

That dress was like some sort of enchantment.

It made her want to believe extraordinary things could happen to ordinary people just like her. It made her want to do the most dangerous thing of all.

Trust again. Hope again. Believe again.

"Abby, what's wrong?"

The truth crashed down around her. *She was falling for him.* That's what was wrong.

And he was acting like some benevolent big brother who saw she needed help in the garden and the occasional outing. She yearned for his kisses, for his breath in her ears, for the span of his hands on her waist. Not for swing sets.

"Nothing's wrong. I can't go." She went to shut the door, but his foot was in it. "I'd like to have more done on the dress than I have done."

"Mrs. Blundercow's wedding dress," he guessed. "Can I see it?"

"Pondergrove! No. It's unlucky for a man to see a bride's dress before she does." She adjusted the old myth to meet her needs, knowing he wouldn't know any better.

The actual superstition was that the groom should not see the bride in her dress before the wedding day.

She tried to shut the door again.

"Please?" he said. "Come to the play with me."

She closed her eyes, recognizing what it had cost him to say that.

And suddenly she was ashamed of herself. Was this the legacy of her relationship with Ty? *Protect yourself?*

If she really cared for Shane, if it was more than a passing infatuation, wouldn't it ask more of her? Require more of her? Wouldn't it ask her to give, without thought of receiving? Wouldn't real caring want what was best for him?

Shane was a man who had lost everything that mattered to him. His wife. His unborn child. The dreams they had shared together. Their hopes for the future.

Everything had been taken from him in the blink of an eye.

His grief had made him turn his back on the world.

And now, here he was at her door, tentatively reaching out.

She thought of the last few days. Lunch. Flying the kite. Digging in the garden. Laughing over Tetrazzini. The swing set for Belle. He was saying he was willing to give life a chance again, even after all life had done to him. She wasn't even sure that he knew that was the decision he had made.

But she knew his heart was trying to mend, trying to grow toward the light, even if he did not, and she knew it wasn't his fault she reacted to his muscles the way she did, to his voice, to his eyes resting on her. It wasn't his fault that she fiddled with her hair for too long each day, in case she caught a glimpse of him, and it wasn't his fault that she tried on twelve different shirts before she settled on one that looked just right—as if she looked sexy just by accident.

She could not say no to him.

Her personal feelings and fears aside, he was holding out a fragile thing to her. She had an opportunity to help another human being. Would she say no because there was nothing in it for her?

Is that what she would teach her daughter about life?

"Shane," she said, taking a deep breath. "I'd love to go."

She opened her eyes just in time to see him smile, and in that smile she saw that she had done the right thing. The only thing.

"I'll come down Friday about seven, then."

"All right," she whispered, already wondering what to wear.

Chapter Eight

"Oh, my," said Mrs. Pondergrove, her eyes widening behind her glasses, "that is a very glamorous dress."

"Too bold?" Abby asked nervously. The dress was one she had made some time ago, in a reckless moment. It was patterned after one she had fallen in love with while watching the Grammy Awards on television. The dress wasn't indecent. Not in the least. In fact, it had been relatively simple to make.

It had inch wide straps at the shoulders, and an empire waistline. She'd worn a push-up bra that did turn fact to fiction, but in actual fact it was the skirt of the dress that gave it its magic. The skirt was quite full, and two-layered, the top layer a sheer chiffon that swished sexily around her legs.

And of course, the dress was red. Deep true red. The color of blood and hearts and roses.

She had never worn it. Just had a lot of fun making it. And then she had decided it really wasn't the kind of dress someone's mother wore, so she'd filed it away in the back of her closet.

Why had she chosen it tonight?

Because, altruism aside, she didn't plan to be treated like anybody's sister, that's why. If he wanted to be a Boy Scout, he could go find a granny to walk across the street. Mrs. Pondergrove would accommodate him happily, she was sure.

The dress made her feel sensuous and grown-up, not like someone who spent their days playing patty-cake and singing "the bear went over the mountain." Not just a mother. But a woman.

"Is it too bold?" she asked again. If the dress shouted bold and blazing, what on earth was she going to do if the signal she was sending out was answered?

Mrs. Pondergrove said, "Oh, no. I think it's just right. I used to have a dress similar to that. Electric blue. I used to wear it dancing with my Alf."

"Is that Mr. Pondergrove?"

"It is. The best man God ever created. We had so many wonderful years together. He's gone now."

"I'm sorry. Has it been long?"

"Several years. Please don't be sorry. When I see the way so many relationships go, I feel very privileged to have known the joy of loving a man so completely. It's a joy I would like for everyone in the world to know. There is no richness like the richness of sharing a beautiful friendship and love with your husband." She said this so wistfully.

So, Abby thought, it really was out there. Not just the stuff of poetry and novels, but a real thing, that real people experienced. A love that survived the years, growing stronger and richer and deeper.

"Do you think you'll ever remarry?" Abby asked.

"Oh, I don't think so. Jordan Hamilton has other ideas, but really, it's preposterous to think of people our age falling in love."

"I don't think it is," Abby said gently. She liked the idea of someone wooing Mrs. Pondergrove. "I think Jordan Hamilton is very handsome, and extremely distinguished."

"Oh, posh," Mrs. Pondergrove said, but she blushed. "Red suits you. Such a passionate color."

"Oh. I'm not sure if that's the signal I want to give."

"Dear, if it isn't, there's something wrong. Perhaps you might want to consider religious life. A nun."

Abby laughed. "I don't know how Belle would fit in at the convent."

"It's not just that Mr. McCall is good-looking," Mrs. Pondergrove continued. "He's decent. Not one of these alley cat kind of men."

"How did you know I was going out with him?"

"Just a guess, dear. I really would have had to have been quite a bit blinder than I am to miss the chemistry between the two of you the last time I was here."

"Chemistry?" Abby squeaked. "You could see it?"

"I've always prided myself on being able to see what others can't always see. Jordan doesn't approve. He calls it meddling in other people's lives."

"How do you know that Shane isn't, um, one of those alley cat kind of men?" She wanted so badly to be able to take her word for it. One thing she did not need was another alley cat kind of man.

"I can tell by looking at him, of course. As I said, I see."

Abby wished there was something a little more solid than that.

"I wish I could see so clearly!" she said.

"Ask your heart."

"Well, I did that once before and I was wrong."

"My dear, you couldn't have possibly asked your heart, because one's heart is never wrong in such matters."

"Well, mine was."

"Something may have been," Mrs. Pondergrove said stubbornly, "but not your heart. For instance, maybe your ego chose the man you are talking about. Maybe he was handsome and dashing and the boy that all the girls talked about. And maybe you thought if he would love you, that would make you feel worth more."

"Good grief," Abby said with the shock of recognition.

"There he is now. Hello, Mr. McCall."

Abby whirled to see Shane leaning lazily on the door-frame. She had not bothered to shut the door to her suite behind Mrs. Pondergrove.

"Mrs. Pondergrove. Abby."

Abby's mouth dropped open. This was not even the same man who ran around the house and yard in his shorts and T-shirt. Shane looked sophisticated and suave in a beautifully cut pair of dark slacks, a white shirt, a silk tie and a dark, expensive suit jacket.

She had never once imagined him in a bigger world, but now that she saw just how he would look in it she felt a little knife of fear. Every woman would react to him just as she was. A sudden quickening of the heart, a sudden slickness at the palms, and sudden hope flickering in the region of the heart.

The question was, how would he react to them?

His eyes rested on her. One of his eyebrows shot up.

"You look stunning," he said, a funny rasp in his voice.

There. She'd accomplished just what she wanted. Only now that she had, it was just as she'd suspected. She didn't have a clue what to do with it, how to turn it to her advantage, how to be the only woman who appealed to him. She doubted if the way to accomplish that was to pick up the white shawl beside her and wrap it primly around her bosom, but that is what she did anyway.

"Thank you," she said stiffly. "Mrs. Pondergrove, if Belle wakes up, she may just want her soother popped back in her mouth."

"You're not to give her another thought," she was ordered sternly by the old woman.

Shane took Abby's hand, tucked it inside his, and ushered her out the door.

"You look gorgeous," he said.

"So do you."

He took one look at her heels, and led her over to his vehicle, a sports utility. "I don't think we'll walk tonight."

She wanted to protest that it would be a beautiful night for a walk, the sea breeze crisp, the light beginning to change to twilight. Besides, it would let her hang on to this moment of intertwined hands for a little longer.

But her own shoes had betrayed her. She was paying a big price to be three inches taller than God had made her.

He opened the door for her, something Ty had never done. The vehicle was very high off the ground, and hard to navigate in the skirt. Suddenly, she felt ridiculous, like she was not even the same person that she had been a few hours ago.

"You don't look like the same person who was pulling worms out of Belle's mouth a few days ago."

When he said it like that, she was able to see it was funny, in a way, and she relaxed. How had he known exactly what to say to make her feel more at ease, more like herself?

"You don't exactly look like the same guy who was on the other end of that shovel either. In fact, I think this is the first time I've ever seen you with your legs covered up."

"Single men. I'm afraid we're notorious for finding what's comfortable and staying in it. Longing for our favorite sweats when we have to put them in the laundry, like little boys having their security blankets washed."

She laughed at the picture he had created. It was ludicrous to think of him pacing back and forth at the laundromat while his favorite shorts went through the rinse cycle.

They arrived at the theater in very short order. Like most of the Miracle Harbor businesses it was on the town's main street, facing out toward the ocean.

It was obviously a very old building that had been beautifully refurbished. She admired the marble tile and the rich burgundy draperies and carpeting in the lobby as they came in.

She also noticed the cream of Miracle Harbor seemed to be out in full force. The lobby was packed with extremely well-dressed people socializing.

"I didn't know this many suits existed in this town," Shane muttered, taking her elbow and propelling her through the thronged lobby. "Have you ever seen a person in this town in anything more dressy than brand-new Levis jeans?"

Never mind the suits, she thought with a gulp. She was suddenly glad she had put on the dress she had, because there were some gorgeous gowns in that lobby, and some gorgeous women tucked into them. Even so, she was suddenly aware her outfit was homemade and she wondered if it showed.

She found herself stealing a look at Shane's face as a woman went by them in a short, sequined black dress that looked like a tube. It could be made with a single seam, she thought.

He didn't even notice! His eyes were fastened on the draped entry to the main theater, his mission to get there, nothing detracting him from that.

Each time they went by a beautiful woman, she stole another look at him. He seemed oblivious to the looks he garnered. Looks of interest, ranging from mild to plain old predatory, looks that sized her up...and put her down.

Ty would have been in his glory. Saying low pitched flirtatious hellos to complete strangers, sending a wink here and there, stopping to talk, his eyes doing a quick and sultry inventory of everything on display.

Shane got them across the room and into the darkened theater in record time. He had not returned one smile.

"I'm sorry," he muttered, when he'd found their seats. "You probably guessed I don't like crowds much."

It touched her that he had overcome this aversion to escort her. What had made him think of the theater if he didn't like crowds?

"Don't you enjoy seeing all the different ways people are dressed?" she asked. In their short dash across the lobby, she had seen fifty dresses that she would just love to attempt to sew. She reminded herself, sternly, that since this was the first occasion she'd had to wear the one she had on, she didn't need anymore fancy dresses cluttering up her closet.

He actually looked surprised at the notion. He gazed at her thoughtfully. "Well, the men are all dressed pretty much the same. And why would I find the women interesting? I'm with the most beautiful woman in Miracle Harbor. And I knew that before you put on that dress. I'd like to see how many of them looked great just goofing off in the garden."

He said that matter-of-factly, then picked up his program and began to read it.

She stared at him, flabbergasted. He had just told her she was beautiful, the most beautiful woman in Miracle Harbor, and now he was reading his program.

At first, she didn't know what to think. If he really believed that, why wasn't he engrossed in her?

But then suddenly it occurred to her that it just confirmed what she already suspected about him.

He was not a man of superficial passions. How things—or women—looked would not sway him. He had a different kind of strength than any she had ever seen before, deeper, cleaner, infinitely more appealing.

It was, she knew, with sudden insight, that very strength that held him prisoner right now. He believed, with his whole heart and soul, that he had let down someone who loved him. Failed her. And he could not forgive himself for that.

Sighing, she took his hand in hers, ignored his eyes on her face, and looked to the front. His hand in hers felt right. It was that uncomplicated, and that beautiful, and that frightening. She belonged with Shane McCall.

Would he ever see that?

* * *

The play was a light, competently produced comedy if Shane judged it by the amount of laughter around him. The truth was that he had trouble concentrating on it. He liked the way her hand felt in his. He liked the way the shadows in the darkened room played with the blond of her hair. He liked the view he had out of the side of his eye, especially after she took off the shawl and put it in her lap. Her shoulders were even better than her belly button.

The dress seemed to him to be an engineering marvel far worthier of his attention than the play.

Damn. He'd gone and told her she was beautiful. The most beautiful woman here. It was only the truth, but somehow he'd wished even as those words were slipping off his tongue, that he could pluck them out of the air and stuff them back in his mouth.

Until he'd seen the light come on in her eyes, and known, somehow, he had stumbled onto what she most needed to hear.

Why would she doubt that about herself?

He had not missed her anxious looks every time one of those ladies in the slippery dresses had glided by. What had caused that kind of insecurity in her?

The whole play had drifted away while he contemplated these weightier issues.

"Did you like it?" she asked, slipping the shawl back over her shoulders, and rising as the last of the applause died down.

"Sure," he said, hoping to hell she wasn't referring to his enjoyment of her décolleté. Why was it, more than any woman ever had, she reminded him a pervert was alive and well and living inside him? "Did you?"

"It was fun."

On a hunch, he asked her which part she had liked best. Ha. She couldn't answer him, and she didn't even have an astonishing red dress to use as an excuse.

The crowds had pretty much dispersed when they got outside.

"Do you want to go for a quick bite to eat?" he asked. "A drink?"

Her hand was still in his. Something about that felt so right.

"No," she said. "Shane, look at the moonlight on the waves."

He looked across the street to the wide stretch of beach. Beyond it, the ocean was restless.

"The waves look like showgirls," she said, "in frothy feathery hats."

Not saying anything, he guided her across the street. She kicked off her shoes as soon as they hit the sand, wriggled her stocking clad feet, tilting her head back to look at the heavens. He wanted to kiss her throat.

He wanted to kiss the living daylights out of her.

Instead he said, "What's the story with Belle's father?" Once a cop always a cop. There was a mystery about that insecurity she felt, and he damned well intended to sniff it out.

She pulled her hand from his and wrapped her shawl around her, headed down the shoreline. He walked beside her. After awhile he took off his shoes, too. Just when he thought his question had been far too personal, she answered him.

"He was never interested in Belle. To be truthful, he was never that interested in me. I mean he was interested in all women, but not me in particular."

"Snake," Shane said. That explained it, all right.

"There seems to be lots of snakes in the woods," she said.

"Yeah, that's true."

"And along comes Little Red Riding Hood."

"I think it was wolves she had to be worried about. But you got the color of the dress right."

"You're not one of them, are you Shane McCall?"

"One of those wolves or snakes young ladies in red dresses have to be so wary of?" he asked carefully

She nodded, her eyes huge on his face. Moonlight did wonderful things to her eyes. She looked away from him at the waves breaking on shore.

In this moment, he wanted to be everything she wanted him to be. But he knew he was not. "Not the kind you're talking about, anyway."

"I don't believe you are any kind of a snake."

"And what about a wolf?" he asked, trying to kid, wanting desperately to steer her away from where he knew this was going.

"No, Shane, not a wolf either. I think you are the rarest of things—a man worthy of a woman's trust."

Suddenly the truth about him was there, clawing at his throat, begging to get out. Well, why not? That should kill the light in her eyes quick enough. Destroy her illusions.

"I think maybe you've got me wrong, Abby."

"I don't think so." She said it stubbornly, as if she could know these things.

He knew he was going to tell her the truth, whether to kill her illusions or to get it off his own conscience he wasn't quite sure.

"Remember I told you my wife died falling down the stairs?"

"Yes, I remember."

"I was supposed to be home that day. I got called into work. She didn't want me to go. She was so nervous about having a baby. She was scared to death something would happen to me. She was worried I'd get into a situation that wouldn't be easy to get out of, and that the baby would be born without me being there. We'd taken those classes together. Prenatal." He laughed softly. "I can't tell you how much I hated them.

"Anyway, I didn't take her seriously. I told her I could be home in the blink of an eye, if I needed to. But we weren't expecting the baby for another full month. I thought she was being silly."

He watched out of the corner of his eye as she put her shawl in the sand, then sat on it. She patted the place beside her, and he hesitated and then sat down. His shoulder grazed hers.

"If I'd been there," he said, "if I had stayed home, if only I had recognized she wasn't being silly. Maybe she'd had a premonition. Maybe she *knew* something was going to happen, and tried to tell me, and I wasn't listening. Not in the right way."

She leaned her head into him. He could feel her trembling, and he glanced down at her. She was crying, silently, silver tears washing down her cheeks.

"It won't help if I tell you it wasn't your fault," she whispered.

"No."

She was silent.

"I even regret that I hated the stupid classes. If people knew the clock was ticking, they'd treasure everything. Every breath, every *cleansing breath.*"

"Oh, Shane." She picked up a corner of her shawl and wiped her eyes on it.

Well, once a jerk, always a jerk. Here he had a beautiful woman on the beach, and he'd made her cry. His intention tonight had been to make her laugh, to lighten her load.

"I can only tell you what I see now," she said, her voice composed, soft, lovely with the swish and crash of the waves as a backdrop. "Not perfect. Capable of making mistakes. Strong, too. Maybe strong enough to forgive yourself, one day. I hope so."

She was crying for him. Because he was hurt, and she could feel his pain, almost in a way he had not allowed himself to feel it.

"Don't cry."

"It's just so sad, Shane. You would have felt the same way if she had been hit by a car, or if it had happened while she was having the baby, wouldn't you?"

He thought about that. "Yeah. I guess."

"You see, it's why you picked the job you do. You want to protect. Be in control. Be in charge."

It was making him very uneasy that she could see him so clearly.

"But you see, Shane, there are some things human beings are not in charge of, no matter how much they want to be. And life and death is one of those things."

"I guess that's true, isn't it?" But he could feel the reluctance in him to admit the truth of it, even though he knew his heart could not begin to heal as long as he blamed himself.

"Shane?"

"Hmm?"

"Would she have wanted you to feel like this?"

"Good God, no. She would have been madder than hell at me."

"Then maybe the only thing you have left to give

her, the only way you can truly honor her memory is to be the man she would have wanted you to be. If she loved you, she wanted you—wants you—to be free. And happy. And open to all life has to offer you."

"And now I'm chained by cynicism, and unhappy and closed."

She didn't have to say anything. He recognized the truth about himself. And knew she was absolutely right.

What had he done in his life to deserve two women who were capable of seeing him so clearly?

And what had he done to deserve this second chance? To feel again, the exhilarating ride of falling over a cliff into a woman's eyes?

He touched his lips to the top of her head. Her hair was soft and silky and smelled of meadows ripe with buttercups.

She tilted her head up.

And he took what she offered. He took her lips and tasted them. Really tasted them. The sweetness, the innocence there, despite her having borne a child, that was like nothing he had ever experienced before.

The thundering of the sea faded, replaced by the thundering of his heart.

He could taste a hint of salt on her lips.

He let his calloused hands explore the sweet curves of her shoulders, the exquisite softness of her skin, the tender curve of her neck.

He wanted to pull her down in the sand with him, to let go completely of this demon called control that had run his life.

He wanted to be free and happy and open.

Above all things, he wanted to make love to her.

But not here on a public beach in the sand.

At home, where he could take that dress from her

and drop it to the floor, look at her, taste her, feel her, tumble her backward into his bed.

"Let's go home," he growled.

She stood up, took his hand, and they went together across the sand toward a brand-new future.

A future that twinkled with hope as surely as the stars twinkled in the sky.

Chapter Nine

The drive home gave him time to sober, to pull back
from the intoxicating nearness of her, from the heady
feel of her skin beneath his lips.

On the way home, reality knocked.

Had he made his bed this morning? Left his dirty
clothes on the floor? A friend, well meaning, had sent
him the "Swimsuit Issue" of *Sports Illustrated* last
month. He had no patience with things like that, but
suddenly he wondered where he had tossed it. He didn't
want her to see it. He wanted any thought she had ever
had of him being a pervert to be completely banished.

Reality knocked, and asked him how the hell he
planned to slip her by Mrs. Pondergrove, and how he
felt about that. Sneaking her into his room as if he was
a college freshman in a dorm instead of a full-grown
man, mature and respected.

Reality knocked, and asked him if this is what he
really wanted, not just with his body, but with everything. His mind. His soul. It told him she was not the

kind of girl a man should act out an impulse with. She had been the victim of such behavior once before. He wanted to rip the guy apart with his bare hands, so how could he rationalize what he wanted to do tonight?

The voice of reason calmly asked him about what he was planning to do about tomorrow. Move in with her? Buy her a ring? What?

But as soon as he stopped the vehicle, turned off the key, shifted in his seat and looked at her, he didn't care about any of those things. She wouldn't care if the bed was made. They'd send Mrs. Pondergrove home. He hoped to hell he didn't have to drive her.

And tomorrow? Wasn't there a saying that tomorrow never comes?

He came around and opened her door.

She slipped out and into his arms, her lips finding his, famished.

Kissing, their hunger that of two people who had had nothing to eat and suddenly found themselves at a banquet, they went up the walk.

They stood in the darkness of the porch for the longest time, her giggles breathless as his lips touched the places where that dress ended, growing bolder, the fire in him leaping up, threatening to consume him, and her. The voice of reason had already been consumed.

And then suddenly the light came on and bathed them in a glow that seemed too harsh. The door was thrown open with much more vigor than he would have expected of an old lady. And it was not an old lady who stood there, smiling wickedly at them.

"Hi, honey," she said, "I'm home."

Geez. It was her. Abby. Only slightly different. The hair long and wild, the makeup sophisticated, the eyes dancing with a certain devilment that Abby would never be able to manage. And Abby would never dress like that. The rich white silk blouse, cut low at the front, clinging. Expensive jewelry dripping from every earlobe and finger.

Abby shot him a stunned look. He stepped back from her.

"Brittany," she said, trying for enthusiasm and failing miserably.

She gave him one more look, loaded with regret, before she slipped from his side, opened the screen door that separated her from her sister, and hugged her tight.

"Brittany," she said, collecting herself, "I'm so glad you are here."

He wished he could say the same, only it was impossible. He was not glad she was here, at all.

"Well," Brittany said, squeezing her sister, but raising an eyebrow at him over her shoulder, "my timing seems to be a little off, doesn't it?"

"Oh," Abby said awkwardly. "Brittany, this is Shane McCall."

"And to think I sent you a book on hunting men! Girl, why didn't you tell me you didn't need any help from me?"

Abby's mouth worked soundlessly and she sent her sister a pleading look that the girl managed to ignore entirely.

"Is that what that wedding dress in there is all about? It's gorgeous."

"No!" Abby wailed.

"Gorgeous, just like him. So, is he the one? Give."

Abby was looking at her feet, now, a dejected slump to her shoulders.

Shane felt like he wanted to kill her sister for being so bloody insensitive.

But the sister's next words caught him like a slug to the chin.

"Is he the one you're going to marry so you can keep this darling house for good?"

"Brittany, please," but her voice was faint and fading.

"Oh, God, doesn't he know?"

Heavy silence followed.

"Know what?" he asked.

"Nothing," Brittany said swiftly.

"Abby?" he asked, noting she was trying to become invisible, an impossibility given the style and color of that dress.

Shane suspected she was praying. But he knew no matter how much she hoped the floor was going to rot away and let her fall through it, no matter how preferable dropping into a bed of spiders was to the situation she now found herself in, it was going to happen. She lifted her chin and looked at him.

"This house was given to me as a gift. But it has a condition attached to my keeping it."

Her eyes were pleading with him not to ask.

Why the hell start being a nice guy this late in his development? His honorary halo, awarded to him for his past few days of being Mr. Nice Guy was getting too tight anyway. "What condition is that?"

"I would never get married just to keep a house," she said to him. "Never."

"Married?" he breathed. "Somebody gave you this house, but told you you had to get married to keep it?"

She nodded, embarrassed, looking anywhere but at him.

"Who did that to you?" He felt furious. Not just with her, though he felt that, too.

"I don't know. A stranger."

"Well, I think its a pretty crummy thing to do to someone with a kid to look after." Looking at her, he felt she had been boxed in. What choice did she have? She had Belle to look after, and he'd seen her with Belle. Her child was her first priority. And he admired her for that.

Until now. What if her only interest in him was gaining this house? Dear God, if those kisses had been lies, he would never be able to trust himself, or a woman, again.

Mrs. Pondergrove had edged out into the hallway, and was looking at them anxiously, feeling the tension. "What's a crummy thing to do?" she asked Shane, making him realize he must have raised his voice.

"Give someone a house, but attach a string to it that she has to get married."

"Oh gracious," Mrs. Pondergrove said, obviously shocked. She put her fist up to her mouth and looked at them with worried eyes. "Wouldn't that person have meant well?"

"I doubt it," he snapped. "It's kind of a mercenary thing to do. A marriage for a house." He felt like he was going to explode, and it must have showed judging from all those anxious female eyes fastened to his face.

"Mrs. Pondergrove, I'll drive you home."

"Thank you. That's very kind. But I don't mind walking."

"Just get in the truck." She didn't want to go with him, and he didn't blame her. He realized his tone was more appropriate to a drug bust than a little old lady. Mind you, that's kind of what this was, wasn't it? A bust. The real live motivations coming to the surface. That little number in the red dress wrapping him around her finger so she could have a house. Not that that had anything to do with Mrs. Pondergrove who was now twittering nervously, like a bird without a nest.

"Please allow me to drive you home," he amended. "I've been a policeman my whole adult life. Women are vulnerable at night."

Especially little old ones like her, though he didn't want to frighten her by adding that.

"Oh, all right," she said timidly. "Just let me find my coat. Oh dear. Where's my jacket?"

In a moment her jacket had been found for her, and he had helped her into it, and was escorting her down the walk. This was so far from how he'd planned for the evening to end that he could have laughed. Except that he was so angry.

"Please don't be angry at her," Mrs. Pondergrove said quietly as he pulled away from the curb. "It's not her fault about the condition."

"She could have told me."

"I would think maybe she's a little embarrassed about it."

That dress was not the dress of someone who would be embarrassed by a little something like that. That dress was the dress of someone setting a trap.

"She's so naive," he said. "Whoever is behind that gift will probably come knocking on her door, woo her for a few weeks, drop the question, and that will be that."

He realized his mind was contradicting itself. Seeing her as conniving one minute, and naive the next.

He did not think he had felt so hopelessly confused since—ever.

"I don't think that's what will happen," the old lady said.

Something in her voice made him look at her narrowly. What did she know about it? But she was looking through her handbag, a befuddled expression on her face. She came out with a worn looking package of gum.

"Would you like some?" she offered brightly.

"No."

"Turn left here, dear. There's my house. Right up there."

He pulled to a stop in front of a well-kept little Victorian, and got out to help her out of the vehicle. He ended up practically picking her up to help her down.

Which allowed him to see her face very clearly under the glow of the streetlight.

The old gal looked guilty as hell.

But about what? Well, that was one of his specialties. Finding out things people didn't want him to know. He was writing a whole chapter about prying secrets from people, about investigation. And he intended to get to the bottom of this whole thing. Tomorrow he planned to start asking some tough questions.

For Abby's protection.

Even if she didn't deserve it.

By the time he got home, his resolve was fading. He felt like the black weight was descending on him again. Like he had been allowed to be free of it for a few hours, but now its coming back was all the more painful.

He opened the outer door to the house. The door to her suite was slightly open. He tried to slip by, because he had this awful feeling that even looking at her might disturb his ability to think, his investigative powers.

"Where are you going?" Brit demanded, appearing suddenly in the doorway.

"I live here," he said coolly.

"You live here? With my sister?"

"I'm her tenant. I have an apartment upstairs."

"Her tenant," Brit said, then laughed, and called over her shoulder, "I get a stupid bakery as a gift, and you get a house with him in it? I wonder where I register my complaint?"

She closed the door to Abby's suite.

He went slowly up the stairs, feeling like fifty pound weights had been attached to his ankles. He went into his suite, sought refuge in the familiar order of everything but found none. Of course the bed was made, his laundry was in the hamper, and that magazine was filed somewhere. He closed the door, sank to the floor and stared at his hands.

Come on McCall, he told himself. What was the big surprise? He'd seen that book in her bag on the front seat of her car the first day she'd been here. He'd known she needed someone.

The big surprise was that she had cold-bloodedly been hunting for a husband.

The big surprise was that he thought he was the last person on earth anyone could ever succeed in pulling one over on. Too cynical. Had seen to much, both in his professional life and his personal one.

Ha, ha. Big tough Shane McCall.

But it seemed to be true. The bigger they were, the harder they fell.

He closed his eyes, rested his head in his hands, and tried not to think at all. Not even a little bit.

Now there was something he was good at.

"My, God," Brittany said, the door closed behind her, leaning against it. "That man! He's stunning. I'm so jealous, I could spit.''

''There's nothing to be jealous of. We're just friends.'' Had been friends, Abby thought. She didn't even know if she had that anymore. ''Could we change the subject?''

''All right. I love your dress. That shade of red is so *va-room, va-room.* Where on earth did you find it? It's exquisite.''

''I made it,'' Abby said woodenly. She wanted desperately to be happy to see her sister. But all she could think of was the look on his face when he'd found out the truth.

''Can you make me one? Say in peach? I look stunning in peach.'' She laughed. ''Of course, what I look stunning in, you look stunning in.''

Abby smiled weakly.

''My niece is gorgeous. She seemed to know me. The old gal didn't think I should wake her up, but I didn't think it would hurt. What was her name, Mrs. Poundcake?''

''Pondergrove,'' Abby corrected her, half-heartedly.

''Oh. Right. I guess I'm just thinking of cakes because I got the bakery as my gift. Not exactly my cup of tea, but wait until I tell you some of my plans. I'm actually excited about taking it over.''

''That's wonderful,'' Abby managed to say.

Brittany looked at her closely, and then hit herself on the forehead with the palm of her hand.

''Oh, God, I should have kept my big mouth shut, right? Oh, Abby, I'm sorry. I was trying to make an impression. He's *so* good-looking, I just kind of started to run off at the mouth. I wasn't even thinking what I was saying, just babbling away. I've hurt you.''

"No," Abby said, "Really you haven't. Weren't we going to change the subject?"

"I'm terrible in the sensitivity department, Abby. I am. When my parents kicked me out last year, they said I was a spoiled little rich girl who didn't know the first thing about life, and that it was time for me to learn."

"Your parents kicked you out?" Abby said, managing to rise out of her own pain and confusion. Right underneath Brit's breezy tone, she detected pain.

"After I wrecked my car. They overreacted, I'd say, even if it was the second one I wrecked."

"Wrecked how?" Abby asked.

"Too fast into a corner. I love going fast. Don't you?"

"No," Abby said.

"Well, you wouldn't know it to see the progress you've made with the Hunk of Miracle Harbor. How long have you known him?"

"Not very long," Abby said, but the words sounded oddly false. Because she felt like she had known Shane McCall forever and beyond. "You were telling me about your car."

"Oh, yeah. I wrecked it. Second one. A red Corvette, almost the same color as your dress. Mommy and Daddy had a fit. Sat me down and told me they realized they had been guilty of giving me too much, and that the free ride was over. They cut the purse strings, just like that."

Again, this was delivered in a breezy, I-don't-give-a-damn style, that Abby sensed hid a more sensitive person, after all.

"Anyway, I was getting a little desperate. I've sold some jewelry to make ends meet. I'd applied for all kinds of jobs, but I never got asked for an interview."

Abby detected hurt and confusion in the words.

"But remember when we got our gift, and the lawyer who read it said it was supposed to be the thing we needed most? Well I guess what I needed most was a job. And I got one. And really, I am grateful, Abby. But can you see me icing cakes?"

Abby had to smile despite the terrible pain in her heart. Honestly she could not picture her sister icing a cake.

"But that's enough about me. I want to hear all about you. Start with my beautiful niece. No, start before that. Have you found out why we were split up yet?"

"No. I talked to my Mom—my adopted Mom—several times since all this happened, but if she knows anything she's not saying."

"Well, she has to know something. She didn't find you under a cabbage leaf."

"She said my Aunt Ella made all the arrangements."

"Ask her then!"

"She's been dead for thirteen years."

"Oh, sorry."

"My mother was a nurse at a hospital in Minnesota. She said I was there and she fell in love with me, and found out I needed a home. She had wanted a baby forever. I wasn't exactly a baby, though. I was three when she got me."

"My Mom and Dad said I was just about to turn three when they got me, too. How come you were in the hospital?"

"I don't know about the hospital. I've been wondering about what Corrine said, about our parents being killed in a car accident. Maybe I was in it, too. Do you know how your adopted parents got you?"

"This is awful, but I think my parents bought me."

"What?"

"No kidding. Black market baby. They're not too anxious to talk about it, so I figure something is fishy. I do know they wanted a child desperately. They're not the kind of people to wait for anything if money can buy it. Not that I want to give the impression that they are bad people, because nothing could be further from the truth. But they know money is power and they are not afraid to use it."

"Whatever the reasons we were split up, I'm so glad we were brought together," Abby said. "I can't bring myself to believe that whoever went to all this trouble to get us together had some ulterior motive."

"Well, I'm more than a match for anybody with an ulterior motive. But I don't know about you. Gosh, you're sweet." She laughed. "You're the sweet one. I'm the wild one. What do you suppose sister Corrine is?"

"I don't know. I've only talked to her a few times on the phone. She seems—"

"Reticent?" Brittany suggested.

"Exactly." Abby didn't add, *or scared.*

"She told me she was burning the book I sent her. Didn't even want to donate it to the library. Said that would be like spreading poison in drinking water. Do you think that's a little strong?"

Abby found herself laughing, which was amazing, because fifteen minutes ago she had sworn she would never laugh again. "Actually, I don't think that's too strong. Did she tell you when she's coming?"

"She's got commitments that will take her a while to tie up. She's written and illustrated a book. Isn't that adorable?"

"I can't wait to see her book." Abby said. "She's sending me one."

"I have the most wonderful idea," Brit said, Abby realized she was going to have to adjust to these lightening swift changes of topic. Brittany's eyes caught on the wedding dress, being worn by the mannequin in the corner. "Could I try that on?"

Abby turned and stared at the dress. The sewing of the dress was completed. She had begun the arduous job of hand beading the bodice a day or two ago. Yet she didn't want her sister to try it on. Why not? It would give her her first real chance to fit the dress, something that was difficult to do with herself. So far, she had been making the dress from her own measurements. But for some reason she had not tried it on, avoided that with her whole heart and soul.

"Please?" Brit said. "Abby, it is so beautiful."

Abby went and took the dress gently from the mannequin. "Come here," she told her sister.

Without a bit of self-consciousness, Brit had stripped down to her bra and panties in a blink. Abby noticed they were exactly the kind of underthings she never wore. Lacy, and brief, sexy.

They slipped the dress over Brit's head. Abby had not yet done the buttons on the back of it, so she pinned her sister into the dress.

It fit perfectly, almost as if it had been made for Brit.

"How do I look?" Brit asked, her eyes shining.

Abby couldn't bring herself to look at her. Instead, she went and got her stand-alone full-length mirror and set it up in front of her sister.

Brit gazed at herself, but her smile became fixed and then faded. Her brow dropped thoughtfully.

"Isn't that funny?" she said. "I love this dress. I mean it is an absolute dream. But I don't like it on me.

It doesn't feel right, somehow. I don't know what it is. Too sweet, maybe. You try it.''

"Oh, no," Abby said, and felt her cheeks flush.

"Come on. It's just a bit of dress-up. The kind of thing we would have done if we had grown up together, up in the attic going through old trunks. Don't be such a stick."

"A stick?"

"A stick-in-the-mud. Try it on. It'll be fun."

Somehow, Abby found herself with the dress in her arms. She wasn't anywhere near as uninhibited as her California sister, so she went into the bathroom to put it on.

It felt like she was slipping into her own skin. There was such a sense of belonging to that dress, as if it was made for her.

She didn't want to look at herself in it, but Brit was outside the door demanding she come out.

Taking a deep breath, she did.

"Oh!" Brit said. "My sister is an angel. I feel like I'm going to cry. I have never in my life seen anything so beautiful." She took Abby's hand and pulled her over to the mirror.

"Open your eyes, silly girl."

Abby opened one eye. Just a peek. And then she opened both of them.

The dress was everything she had known it would be, and more. It fit her perfectly, falling in exquisite lines and making her look like a princess.

It wasn't just a dress. It was a dream come true. It was an enchantment. In her eyes was the deep and contented glow of a woman in love.

But she reminded herself, this dream took two.

And her last look at Shane tonight had not boded well

for her future. Certainly not her future in terms of a dress like this one.

She turned and darted back toward the bathroom, feeling like she was going to cry. The dress made her feel so right. So womanly, so full of hopes and dreams.

But that wasn't reality.

Reality and fantasy had just collided and it was terribly painful.

When she emerged from the bathroom, her face scrubbed free of any remaining signs of tears, her sister was waiting.

"This was my wonderful idea, before I got sidetracked by the dress. Lend me some of your pajamas. I left my bag at the hotel. We'll have a pajama party and talk all night. Just like sisters. I just can't wait to find out every single thing about you."

To Abby that sounded far preferable to spending the evening by herself going over what might have been if Brittany had not flung open the door.

Brit wrinkled her nose at the flannel button-up pajamas she was handed.

"Girl, have you ever heard the word sexy?"

"I'm from Chicago," Abby reminded her. "It's cold there at night. You can't sleep in lace baby-dolls."

"I didn't realize you slept outside in Chicago," her sister teased her, unselfconsciously throwing off her clothes once more and donning the pajamas.

Soon they were in Abby's bed talking, and whispering, laughing.

"I can't believe you're afraid of spiders," Brit said. "I just can't believe it."

"Ever since I can remember."

"Me too. I fainted at my high school grad because a spider walked across the collar of the boy in front of me. I blamed it on the heat, of course. Imagine a girl as notorious for her reckless spirit as me being afraid of something so silly.''

"Do you think something happened to us? Before we were separated? Do you think Corrine is afraid of spiders?''

"Let's call and ask her!''

"No! It's late, Brit.''

"Oh, she won't care.''

"We'll call her tomorrow.''

"Well, all right, but I'd rather know tonight.''

Abby realized her sister was a person who had never once considered the possibility of putting someone else's needs ahead of her own.

And yet despite that she was so likable. So irrepressible. So spirited, so funny. Abby felt like she had known her forever. Loved her forever.

What Abby didn't know was that the register above her bed was not a heat duct. That many years ago, a hole had been cut in the floor to let more heat up into the chilly upstairs. The register was strictly for cosmetic purposes.

Shane McCall, lying sleepless in his bed, heard every word of her life story.

Chapter Ten

After a long time, their voices, Abby's and Brittany's, wafting up to him from that register right under his bed, grew husky and then faded.

He should feel guilty. Listening in on them. But what was he supposed to do? Pound on the floor with his foot?

Why should a man feel guilty for lying in his own bed?

The truth was he had felt guilty since Stacey died. Felt he should have been there, could have stopped it.

He remembered Abby's voice on the beach soft in the velvet of the night, as she found the truth; that he would have felt he had failed no matter how his wife had died. And then Abby had found that other truth.

He had not honored who Stacey was, or the love they had celebrated together, by turning his back on life.

He could only honor what had been, by allowing the man Stacey had helped him to become, to come out.

And that man had, among other things, always known the truth, and always acted with complete integrity.

There was a truth in this dark bedroom with him tonight.

It was the truth of his own loneliness.

The truth of the life he was leading, bereft of human emotion.

It was the truth that she had changed that. Abby. Abby had carried sunshine into this cave he had ensconced himself in.

There, in the darkness of his room, with the clock ticking off the minutes after three and the foghorn penetrating the thick white mist outside his window, he admitted the one thing to himself that he found the most difficult to admit. The thing he had been trying to outrun since she had first landed on his doorstep in the middle of a foggy night just like this one.

The thing he had not recognized even when he had taken Abby in for the night, and then offered to look after her car, and then offered to dig the garden, and find her a tenant.

He'd been looking after her.

And it wasn't that she needed looking after.

It's that he had wanted to do it. It had made him feel alive again to have her to care about, her and Belle.

With his whole heart and soul, he wanted to look after her, care for her, protect her, be there for her.

And there was a word for that one thing that he didn't want to admit.

But he wasn't going to say it.

Ever.

He woke the next morning feeling like he had not slept, feeling groggy and out of sorts. He glanced at the clock beside his bed. According to *his* schedule, which was about to be reimplemented in a big way, he had ten minutes left before the kitchen was hers.

He pulled on his running shorts and a T-shirt and headed down the stairs.

After a quick breakfast drink he planned to run. And run and run. To run until his thoughts ran clear of her, like rust clearing from a tap that had not been turned on for a long time. And when he got back he was going to begin making inquiries.

If he found out someone with an evil motive had given her this house he was not sure if he could be trusted to deal with it maturely.

Even if the motive was not evil—just a little off-color—he was not sure what he would do.

Still, it was puzzling. Her sister had mentioned a bakery. Was marriage a condition on that, too? Her sister had looked like about the least likely person in the whole world to run a bakery. And if marriage was a condition for her, too, it would mean that Abby had not been targeted.

Her sister would be more suited, it seemed to him, to a little fashion shop, or a cosmetics business. Were there fingernail shops? Her sister's fingernails had been long and spangled with bright nail polish.

He slammed to a halt at the kitchen door. *She* was in there. Abby. Even though she knew it was his time. Her back to him she was dressed in that backward ball cap and those too big jeans and the white sweater which was too small and showed the slender line of her back to him before it disappeared inside the waistband of her jeans.

Was she trying to push him over the edge of his control?

If so, she had succeeded.

Because that word that he had been avoiding so stringently, suddenly flashed across his brain in neon, ten-foot high letters.

Love.

He loved her.

Damn it all. He loved her. She may have tricked him and manipulated him, and it didn't seem to make a damn bit of difference.

He ordered himself to turn away. To go down the hall and out the door. He could pick up breakfast at the cafe. And get a newspaper at the same time. He didn't care if he had to rent a motel. He was getting out of here.

But his mind disobeyed his order.

He crossed the space of the kitchen on tiger-quiet feet, came up behind her, grabbed her shoulder and whirled her around.

He didn't even really see the look on her face.

He kissed her—hard and long, a kiss loaded with all his frustration and humiliation, a kiss that punished as much as anything else.

Punished her for his own weakness. Punished her for making him hope again.

It was penetrating his senses that something was very wrong here.

Very wrong.

It didn't feel right. He didn't feel that overwhelming sweetness Abby made him feel. He didn't feel like he was in a meadow full of buttercups.

This kiss felt like a lie.

He felt like he was kissing a tiger. He noticed the fingernails digging into his biceps.

Wrong girl his brain shouted at him.

Just a moment too late.

Because he heard the cry of dismay from behind him, fought his way loose of the arms that entwined him and whirled.

To see Abby standing behind them, her fist stuffed in her mouth, tears shining in her eyes. She whirled and was gone in the blink of an eye.

He swore, then looked at her sister. "How dare you?"

"How dare *me?* I wasn't the one who started that, buster."

"Well, you sure didn't finish it. I thought you were her."

"And I was supposed to know that?"

"You're wearing her clothes!"

"Mine are at the hotel."

"What would I kiss you for? You're a complete stranger."

"That didn't matter a fig the last time she found herself a guy. And just for your information, that's why I didn't slug you. I wanted to know if you were like him. She couldn't survive another him." The anger suddenly faded from Brit's face. "But you aren't like him, are you?"

"Like who?"

"That creep she tangled up with. Ty something. She told me all about it last night. He preyed on her innocence. When you started kissing me, I admit, at first, I kind of thought—Wow! Nice way to start the day. Even though it was exactly like that wedding dress, and didn't quite fit me. When you started kissing me, I thought she'd done it again, poor thing. Found a man who couldn't be happy with just her."

"That man would be a complete fool," he bit out.

"I think maybe you need to tell my sister that."

"All your sister wants from me is a house."

"Now who's being the complete fool?"

He stiffened under the criticism.

"You want to believe that," Brit said softly.

Truth, another truth, hitting even harder and closer to home this time. Loving was a risk. A risk that could end in a moment, that held no guarantees, that could leave a strong man in tatters. He was looking, almost desperately for one last out, before he threw himself over that cliff again.

Brittany wasn't letting him off the hook, either. "Do you believe a woman who just wanted a house would have reacted to you and I having a little wake-up kiss the way she did?"

It felt like the sun was coming out, piercing the dark clouds that had inhabited his soul for so long, piercing them, and then evaporating them. He ran out of the kitchen.

"Abby!" He pounded on her door. "Let me in."

Silence.

He considered kicking the door down, but tried the handle instead. The door whispered open. "Abby?"

No answer. He ran from room to room looking for her. But the feeling of emptiness, his voice echoing back to him, told him she was gone.

He ran out into the street, looked both ways. He could see her, pushing her stroller, practically running, nearly two blocks away.

He ran after her, sprinting, finally pulled up beside her, puffing.

The tears were streaming down her cheeks as she walked quickly, her chin tilted at a haughty angle.

"Abby!"

"Get away from me."

"Let me explain."

"I have heard all the explanations in my life I ever want to hear. I saw what I saw."

The baby was crying, too, her head crooked around the side of the stroller, looking back at her mother.

"Abby!"

"Get away from me you, you pervert."

This was so much like their first meeting it was sending shivers up and down his spine. Belle was absolutely howling now, attracting all kinds of attention.

"I thought she was you. I thought your sister was you."

She faltered for the first time, shot him a glance from under her lashes, then picked up her pace. "Sure."

"I did. She was wearing your baseball cap. She was wearing your clothes. She looks exactly like you, for Pete's sake."

She stopped walking and looked at him. "Her hair's different than mine."

"She had it tucked up under that ball cap. She looked exactly like you." He took a deep breath. "But she doesn't feel like you."

"What?"

He was really working on getting himself slapped today. "Not *that* way. Geez, who's the pervert here?"

"You are."

"When I kissed her, I didn't feel the way I felt when I'm around you."

He had her attention now.

"I didn't feel like the blood running through my veins had turned to fire, and I didn't feel as though my heart was going to crash right out of my chest."

Even the baby had stopped crying.

"I didn't feel like it was *true*. When I kissed you last night it felt like the truest thing I'd ever done."

"It did?"

"Abby, I didn't feel alive when I kissed your sister. That's what I feel when I'm with you. Alive. Like the life force is sizzling through my veins, like I want to be alive."

"Shane, what are you saying?"

"I'm in love with you."

A light came on in her face, then died just as quickly. "You are not. You want me to have that house don't you? You're carrying this big brother thing to a ridiculous extreme."

"Big brother thing?"

"You know. Giving me outings. Building Belle swing sets. Protecting me from spiders and unworthy tenants."

"I have sure as hell never felt like your big brother!"

"You haven't? You haven't just decided you'll help me get the house, just like you helped me with everything else?"

"I don't give a damn about that house."

"I don't either."

He cocked his head at her.

"I mean obviously, I like the house. And obviously I'd like to have a house to raise my daughter in, but Shane, if you felt for one second that I only fell in love with you because of that house, I'd give it away, to the first person who wanted it. The girl with the purple hair and the iguana. I'd walk away from it in a second."

"What did you just say?"

"That I'd walk away from the house tomorrow."

"No, before that."

"That I'd give to the girl with the iguana."

"No, before that."

She suddenly was looking everywhere but at him. "I love you," she whispered. "I never meant to fall in love with you, or anybody. I wasn't going to get married to keep that house. I couldn't."

"But if love came along?"

"I don't think," she whispered, "it's a very good idea to say no, when love comes along."

"You know something, darlin', I don't think it is either."

"Oh, Shane, I need you to kiss me."

"No."

"Please?"

"No."

"Why?"

"Because I know where that kiss will go. Right up the steps to my apartment. And, Abby, that's not what I want from you."

"It's not?"

He shook his head. "I want it to be true. And deep. And committed. I want it to be forever. I want to do the right thing always, and be the best man, always. And that doesn't mean sneaking you up the stairs to my room."

"What does it mean?"

"It means marching you down the aisle, with the whole world looking on. It means you wearing a beautiful dress, and carrying a bouquet of flowers."

She laughed through her tears. "Shane, you hate crowds."

"It won't matter to me if there are a million people in that room. I'll only be able to see one of them. You. I want to marry you. So I can wake up beside you always. So that I know those songs I hear you singing are because of the joy I've put in your heart. So that when I think of growing old I feel this wonderful anticipation. So that I can be a daddy to Belle, and a few more just like her.

"I want to be the very best husband in the whole world. And I don't think that will be very difficult with the very best wife."

She threw herself into his arms, and covered his face and his throat and his ears with kisses.

"I warned you," he growled, then groaned, and returned her kisses, and held her to him.

Belle was standing up in her stroller, crowing, trying desperately to get out. He went over and scooped her up and held her close, and then Abby was nestled into his arms, too.

And then Shane McCall smiled, and felt whole.

"Abby, will you ever forgive me because I asked you to marry me today?"

"I don't think forgiveness will ever be a part of my memories of you proposing to me, Shane."

"It's April Fool's day."

She laughed.

"But this is no joke."

"I know."

"I want you to marry me. I want you to marry me as soon as it can be arranged."

"Yes. And that's no joke, either."

They walked back to the house, shoulder to shoulder, he carrying the baby and she pushing the empty stroller.

Her sister was waiting anxiously on the porch. Brittany looked back and forth between them, and then smiled. "Is it what I think it is?"

Abby smiled shyly. "Shane has asked me to marry him."

"Oh," Brit squealed. "I'm so excited. I want to help plan the wedding! This is so wonderful." And then she flew down the steps and hugged her sister, and Shane and the baby, and his arms went around them all.

His new family.

A brand-new circle of love.

Epilogue

Abby stood in front of the mirror, her breath caught in her throat. The reflection told her dreams did come true, even if she could still hardly believe it. It was the first time she had ever tried on the completely finished dress.

"Mrs. Pondergrove, how can I ever thank you?" Mrs. Pondergrove had given her the dress. Given it to her, a virtual stranger. "Of course, I'll refund your money."

Mrs. Pondergrove looked insulted. "My dear, the look on your face is thanks enough. Besides, as the dress got closer to being done, it didn't feel quite right. Not for the woman I'm having it made for. In a week or two, maybe I can drop by with the new dress I've found. From a photograph in a magazine. It's truly lovely."

"I can't wait," Abby said sincerely.

But she knew she wasn't talking about the dress at

all. She was talking about life, stretching in front of her, a glorious adventure to be shared with a glorious man.

Her life, suddenly, everything every woman always dreams her life will be.

"Abby," Brit said catapulting through the door, beautiful in her peach bridesmaid's dress, "do you have it on?"

She skidded to a halt, and her eyes filled with tears. "I have never," she whispered, "seen anything as beautiful as you."

Abby smiled. "Take a look in the mirror, sister."

Corrine came in, quieter, her face glowing. Her peach dress would not have looked out of place at a fashion show. When she saw Abby, her eyes filled with tears, too.

"Stop it, both of you," Abby said sternly. "You'll get me going and nothing will ruin this dress quicker than a few tear stains."

"I have to get it out of my system," Brit insisted, dabbing at her eyes with a hanky, "Or I'll be crying at the wedding and spoil all your pictures. I can't believe Saturday is almost here. How did it come so quickly? I'm a nervous wreck. Abby, how can you look so serene?"

"Because you've looked after everything. I don't have a single thing left to worry about."

"Corrine, that reminds me," Brit said anxiously, "we still have to cover Belle's stroller in white and put the flowers on it. And how are we going to keep her dress clean until we get her into the church? And she won't let me put flowers in her hair!"

"You worry too much," Corrine said, with a tolerant smile.

"No, I don't! You need someone like me to worry. Then everything gets done."

Abby laughed, and she noticed, happily, that Corrine did, too. She thought maybe Corrine's life had not had enough laughter in it.

"Well, enough of the fashion show, ladies," Brit announced. "I have to get over to the church and see how I'm going to fasten the sprigs on the altar. Daisies and babies breath, with a single rose in the center of each arrangement."

For a strange moment, Abby felt transported to the church. It was as if she had walked through the doors. In her mind's eye, she saw herself, going up the aisle in her long white dress, the train floating behind her. The pews each had a bow, just as Brit had described. Spring flowers cascaded out of huge vases on the low stairs leading to the altar.

But the church was empty, save for herself.

And him.

Shane was standing at the altar. As she came down the aisle, it seemed as though he was talking to someone, but there was no one there.

And then he heard her.

And turned.

And the light in his face was what she had always known it could be. The pain of his past had been transformed into strength. She did not know what he had been before, but she knew he was more now than he had been then.

Wiser. More tender. Stronger.

One of those rare men who knew each moment was a miracle. She knew, as he took her hand, she was in the presence of the greatest of all miracles.

Love.

"I thought you said crying would ruin your dress," Brit said. Her sister came and gently wiped the tears from her cheeks. Abby gazed into her sister's eyes and recognized the beginning of a transformation here, too. She opened her arms.

And then all three sisters were holding each other, crying softly, laughing, and wiping tears away.

When they let go of each other Abby saw that Mrs. Pondergrove had quietly slipped away.

Abby looked at her sisters, and felt again the great and abiding presence of the miracles in her life. "Brit, you were right," she said softly. "Peach is your color. Our color. And you were right to make each of these dresses just a wee bit different, like your personalities. You two will be dancing until dawn."

"Oh, God," Brit said, "I don't believe this. In between planning the wedding and getting ready for my bakery's grand reopening, I completely forgot. I don't have a date for the dance. I can't believe this. Me without a date!"

Abby exchanged a look with Corrine over the top of Brittany's head. "What do you think sisters are for?" Abby asked her, softly, and then linking arms the three sisters walked toward the future.

* * * * *

THE WEDDING LEGACY
continues next month
with Brittany's story!

Look for

THE HEIRESS TAKES A HUSBAND

by Cara Colter
Silhouette Romance 1538

Here's a sneak preview...

Chapter One

Once the bride and groom's first dance began, Brittany focused intently on the couple who held center stage. She was not sure she had ever seen such a beautiful sight.

Her sister, Abby, the train of her long ivory wedding dress held up from sweeping the floor by a lace loop attached to her wrist, was dancing her first dance as Mrs. McCall. She and her husband, Shane, moved around the room with the grace of two people who had been born to dance together.

There was something in the way they were looking at each other that made Brit want to believe all over again in the possibility of fairy tales. Happy endings. True love.

Her sister and her new husband danced as if they were alone in the room. The light that shone out of their eyes combined wonder and tenderness and passion to such a degree it made a lump rise in Brittany's throat.

Be happy, she ordered herself sternly, taking another

quick, soothing gulp of the champagne, especially when
it felt like tears pricking at the back of her eyes were
going to fall. As if she'd ever cry in front of *him*.

"I think it's our turn," Mitch said now, turning to
her.

His voice was deep and sexy and full of authority.
He was standing, his hand held out to her. He was such
a commanding figure. He loosened his tie, and she could
see the strong column of his throat, the beginning of
springy, dark hairs on his chest.

It would be nice if he was asking her to dance out of
anything but a sense of duty, but of course that wasn't
the case. The rest of the wedding party was joining the
bride and groom on the dance floor.

Brittany put her hand in Mitch's.

A shock of awareness shivered through her as his
hand, warm and dry and infinitely strong, closed around
hers.

He danced very properly. No pulling too tight and
groping for him. A good size gorilla could have inserted
itself in the space between them. She glanced up at his
face. Remote. Nothing in it to suggest he shared her
feelings of wanting to move a little closer, hold a little
harder.

She decided that it should be made a criminal offense
to be as good looking as he was. The attraction felt like
a beast within her, leaping, hurling itself against a chain,
frothing at the mouth, completely ignoring her feeble
commands to get it in control.

By now, if Mitch had an ounce of good old hot red
blood flowing in his veins, he really should have noticed
how terrific she looked. She decided, abruptly, that she
had had it with Mitch Hamilton and his indifference to

her considerable charms. She felt cut to the quick, hurt beyond reason.

She closed the distance between them, pressed herself into the long length of his body. *Remain indifferent to that,* she challenged him silently.

At first he went very still, and then his hand found the small of her naked back and pressed her into him, even closer. His body was somehow more than she had expected. Harder. She could feel the ridges of his muscles against her own softness.

She hadn't really expected this. To feel as if she had been born to dance with him as surely Abby had been born to dance with Shane. She hadn't expected to feel powerless instead of powerful. Stunned by the feelings shooting through her, and by how vulnerable and needy they made her feel, she committed more deeply and more desperately to convincing him the exact opposite was true.

She kissed him.

At first his lips, tasting of raindrops and honey, were motionless, absolutely still, beneath hers. She registered, in slow motion, how soft they felt when they looked so hard.

Have some pride, she ordered herself, pull away.

But her lips mutinied and were going to do exactly as they pleased. The beast howled happily within her. She wanted to taste Mitch, could not get enough of the taste of him, would forgo champagne forever in favor of this much headier blend. Her lips nudged his, slid across them, coerced, begged.

And when his lips answered, her whole world became sensation, the touch of his lips on hers. Everything and everyone else faded.

The kiss was like a rocket ignited, that soared heavenward and exploded into tiny fragments of delight. She could feel the fragments of that kiss float through her, until not one part of her was left untingling. Her whole body seem to shake and shimmer, to take on an almost iridescent quality.

He pulled away first, and she stared up at him, dazed, shell-shocked from the abrupt transition from one world to the other. His gray eyes were smokey and unreadable, but she could feel the faintest tremor, desire leashed, where his hand rested on the small of her back.

She laughed, shakily. He did not return her smile.

Lightly, she said, "How much do you know about the gifts my sisters and I are receiving?"

"Enough."

You're playing with fire, her mind warned her, while another voice asked: *Why not him?* She needed a husband to receive her inheritance, and he could kiss like a house on fire. That could certainly make up for a lack of a sense of humor. "You might want to think about the conditions of my receiving my gift."

"Conditions?" he asked, his voice smooth and unperturbed, those ocean foam eyes unsettling in their steadiness on her face.

"You know what I'm talking about."

"Oh, *that* condition."

She inclined her head slightly, waited.

He smiled, so slow and sexy it felt like it could make her bones melt. He leaned close to her.

And said, quietly, his breath tickling the nape of her neck, "Not if you were the last woman on earth."

Babies are en route in a trio of
brand-new stories of love found on the
way to the delivery date!

Labor of Love

Featuring

USA Today bestselling author
Sharon Sala

Award-winning author
Marie Ferrarella

And reader favorite
Leanne Banks

On sale this July at your favorite retail outlet!

Only from
Silhouette Books

Where love comes alive™

#1 *New York Times* Bestselling Author

NORA ROBERTS

brings you two tantalizing tales of
remarkable women who live…and love…
on their own terms, featuring characters from

CONSIDERING KATE,

part of her heartwarming Stanislaski saga!

Coming in July 2001

Reflections and Dreams

Some women dream their lives away, but
Lindsay Dunne and Ruth Bannion have *lived*
their dreams. Now they're about to discover passion
and romance beyond even their wildest dreams.

Available at your favorite retail outlet.

Silhouette®
Where love comes alive™

Feel like a star with Silhouette.

We will fly you and a guest to New York City for an exciting weekend stay at a glamorous 5-star hotel. Experience a refreshing day at one of New York's trendiest spas and have your photo taken by a professional. Plus, receive $1,000 U.S. spending money!

**Flowers…long walks…dinner for two…
how does Silhouette Books
make romance come alive for you?**

Send us a script, with 500 words or less, along with visuals (only drawings, magazine cutouts or photographs or combination thereof). Show us how Silhouette Makes Your Love Come Alive. Be creative and have fun. No purchase necessary. All entries must be clearly marked with your name, address and telephone number. All entries will become property of Silhouette and are not returnable. **Contest closes September 28, 2001.**

Please send your entry to: **Silhouette Makes You a Star!**

In U.S.A.	In Canada
P.O. Box 9069	P.O. Box 637
Buffalo, NY, 14269-9069	Fort Erie, ON, L2A 5X3

Look for contest details on the next page, by visiting www.eHarlequin.com or request a copy by sending a self-addressed envelope to the applicable address above. Contest open to Canadian and U.S. residents who are 18 or over. Void where prohibited.

Our lucky winner's photo will appear in a Silhouette ad. Join the fun!

SRMYAS1

HARLEQUIN "SILHOUETTE MAKES YOU A STAR!" CONTEST 1308
OFFICIAL RULES
NO PURCHASE NECESSARY TO ENTER

1. To enter, follow directions published in the offer to which you are responding. Contest begins June 1, 2001, and ends on September 28, 2001. Entries must be postmarked by September 28, 2001, and received by October 5, 2001. Enter by hand-printing (or typing) on an 8 ½" x 11" piece of paper your name, address (including zip code), contest number/name and attaching a script containing 500 words or less, along with drawings, photographs or magazine cutouts, or combinations thereof (i.e., collage) on no larger than 9" x 12" piece of paper, describing how the Silhouette books make romance come alive for you. Mail via first-class mail to: Harlequin "Silhouette Makes You a Star!" Contest 1308, (in the U.S.) P.O. Box 9069, Buffalo, NY 14269-9069, (in Canada) P.O. Box 637, Fort Erie, Ontario, Canada L2A 5X3. Limit one entry per person, household or organization.

2. Contests will be judged by a panel of members of the Harlequin editorial, marketing and public relations staff. Fifty percent of criteria will be judged against script and fifty percent will be judged against drawing, photographs and/or magazine cutouts. Judging criteria will be based on the following:

   • Sincerity—25%
   • Originality and Creativity—50%
   • Emotionally Compelling—25%

   In the event of a tie, duplicate prizes will be awarded. Decisions of the judges are final.

3. All entries become the property of Torstar Corp. and may be used for future promotional purposes. Entries will not be returned. No responsibility is assumed for lost, late, illegible, incomplete, inaccurate, nondelivered or misdirected mail.

4. Contest open only to residents of the U.S. (except Puerto Rico) and Canada who are 18 years of age or older, and is void wherever prohibited by law; all applicable laws and regulations apply. Any litigation within the Province of Quebec respecting the conduct or organization of a publicity contest may be submitted to the Régie des alcools, des courses et des jeux for a ruling. Any litigation respecting the awarding of a prize may be submitted to the Régie des alcools, des courses et des jeux only for the purpose of helping the parties reach a settlement. Employees and immediate family members of Torstar Corp. and D. L. Blair, Inc., their affiliates, subsidiaries and all other agencies, entities and persons connected with the use, marketing or conduct of this contest are not eligible to enter. Taxes on prizes are the sole responsibility of the winner. Acceptance of any prize offered constitutes permission to use winner's name, photograph or other likeness for the purposes of advertising, trade and promotion on behalf of Torstar Corp., its affiliates and subsidiaries without further compensation to the winner, unless prohibited by law.

5. Winner will be determined no later than November 30, 2001, and will be notified by mail. Winner will be required to sign and return an Affidavit of Eligibility/Release of Liability/Publicity Release form within 15 days after winner notification. Noncompliance within that time period may result in disqualification and an alternative winner may be selected. All travelers must execute a Release of Liability prior to ticketing and must possess required travel documents (e.g., passport, photo ID) where applicable. Trip must be booked by December 31, 2001, and completed within one year of notification. No substitution of prize permitted by winner. Torstar Corp. and D. L. Blair, Inc., their parents, affiliates and subsidiaries are not responsible for errors in printing of contest, entries and/or game pieces. In the event of printing or other errors that may result in unintended prize values or duplication of prizes, all affected game pieces or entries shall be null and void. **Purchase or acceptance of a product offer does not improve your chances of winning.**

6. Prizes: (1) Grand Prize—A 2-night/3-day trip for two (2) to New York City, including round-trip coach air transportation nearest winner's home and hotel accommodations (double occupancy) at The Plaza Hotel, a glamorous afternoon makeover at a trendy New York spa. $1,000 in U.S. spending money and an opportunity to have a professional photo taken and appear in a Silhouette advertisement (approximate retail value: $7,000). (10) Ten Runner-Up Prizes of gift packages (retail value $50 ea.). Prizes consist of only those items listed as part of the prize. Limit one prize per person. Prize is valued in U.S. currency.

7. For the name of the winner (available after December 31, 2001) send a self-addressed, stamped envelope to: Harlequin "Silhouette Makes You a Star!" Contest 1197 Winners, P.O. Box 4200 Blair, NE 68009-4200 or you may access the www.eHarlequin.com Web site through February 28, 2002.

Contest sponsored by Torstar Corp., P.O Box 9042, Buffalo, NY 14269-9042.

If you enjoyed what you just read,
then we've got an offer you can't resist!

Take 2 bestselling
love stories FREE!

Plus get a FREE surprise gift!

Clip this page and mail it to Silhouette Reader Service™

IN U.S.A.
3010 Walden Ave.
P.O. Box 1867
Buffalo, N.Y. 14240-1867

IN CANADA
P.O. Box 609
Fort Erie, Ontario
L2A 5X3

YES! Please send me 2 free Silhouette Romance® novels and my free surprise gift. After receiving them, if I don't wish to receive anymore, I can return the shipping statement marked cancel. If I don't cancel, I will receive 6 brand-new novels every month, before they're available in stores! In the U.S.A., bill me at the bargain price of $3.15 plus 25¢ shipping and handling per book and applicable sales tax, if any*. In Canada, bill me at the bargain price of $3.50 plus 25¢ shipping and handling per book and applicable taxes**. That's the complete price and a savings of at least 10% off the cover prices—what a great deal! I understand that accepting the 2 free books and gift places me under no obligation ever to buy any books. I can always return a shipment and cancel at any time. Even if I never buy another book from Silhouette, the 2 free books and gift are mine to keep forever.

215 SEN DFNQ
315 SEN DFNR

Name	(PLEASE PRINT)	
Address		Apt.#
City	State/Prov.	Zip/Postal Code

* Terms and prices subject to change without notice. Sales tax applicable in N.Y.
** Canadian residents will be charged applicable provincial taxes and GST.
All orders subject to approval. Offer limited to one per household and not valid to current Silhouette Romance® subscribers.
® are registered trademarks of Harlequin Enterprises Limited.

SROM01   ©1998 Harlequin Enterprises Limited

MAITLAND MATERNITY

You loved the Maitland family. Now meet the long-lost Maitlands...!

In August 2001, Marie Ferrarella introduces Rafe Maitland, a rugged rancher with a little girl he'd do anything to keep, including—*gulp!*—get married, in **THE INHERITANCE**, a specially packaged story!

Look for it near Silhouette and Harlequin's single titles!

Then meet Rafe's siblings in Silhouette Romance® in the coming months:

Myrna Mackenzie continues the story of the Maitlands with prodigal daughter Laura Maitland in September 2001's **A VERY SPECIAL DELIVERY.**

October 2001 brings the conclusion to this spin-off of the popular Maitland family series, reuniting black sheep Luke Maitland with his family in Stella Bagwell's **THE MISSING MAITLAND.**

Available at your favorite retail outlet.

Silhouette®
Where love comes alive™